Sandy
and the
Black Bag

Books by the same author

Manchineel

NON FICTION
Essential Connections, The How & Why of your personal Energy

Body Mind Connections, The Essential How & Why Book

The Purpose is Love

Sandy
and the
Black Bag

Felicity Rose Mackinnon

ISBN: 978-1-917778-48-0

Author's note

Having created the character of Sandy MacNeil,[1] I decided, after a *lot* of persuasion, that I would have a try at furthering his adventures with material from another, and rather battered manuscript of my Father's that my dear Mama had also given me umpteen years ago; this one based on his years as a doctor after the war. 'Do something with this too, dear,' she'd said.

This was even more anecdotal, haphazard and discursive than his *Manchineel* endeavor so I was really reluctant to try. Could I wrestle mightily with this material and produce a novel of pace and interest, I asked myself? Without Sandy I would not have made the attempt at any time but my daughter's frequent requests to do so however, decided me at least to have a go; it undoubtedly did show what it was like to be in general practice before the National Health Service.

I had my character and now I had my theme.

Well, I like both a challenge and writing, so here is my novel, more a novella. I'd like to think my dear Mama would have been pleased with it; it was her patient typing to Father's dictation that made this book possible.

I have naturally made use of his dialogue, also his locums[2] and 'characters,' based loosely on people he encountered. I have also kept to the facts, as both are most particular to a) the subject and b) the era and its mores.

For the rest, Sandy holds it together and is his own man.

Felicity Rose Mackinnon 2024

[1] Manchineel. (pub: 2024)

[2] from *Locum Tenens* = 'holding the place' i.e. holding the doctor's place while he is ill or on holiday. Usually referred to as the locum: both the doctor filling in *and* the job itself.

▪ Chapter 1 ◀

It was pouring with rain and a stream of it trickled thinly down his neck and off the brim of his hat as Sandy did his best to shoulder his way forward to the Policeman holding back the crowd from the damaged Army lorry.

'Is an ambulance on its way?' he asked, raising his voice with difficulty over the rumble of the passing traffic.

'No, no ambulance yet. It's out on another case and Battersea refused theirs,' the policeman shrugged. 'Not in their area and against regulations! Come over here Doctor.' he added. 'Two of the soldiers in the lorry look in a bad way,' and led Sandy round to the back of the battered vehicle.

Under the very critical eye of the crowd trying to push forward, Sandy followed and looked in at the back. He climbed in and discovered that the two soldiers in obvious pain both had broken bones. He set to, to splint them as best he could. A St John's Ambulance man made a sudden entrance and to his relief was a most welcome assistant.

He offered to stand by till the Ambulance came as Sandy had to get back to the Surgery in Garret Green. He was already an hour late, as on arrival there he'd been immediately called out to an urgent case; then the accident occurred to the lorry. A neighbour had hauled him up the street to the anxious policeman and the chaos on the corner.

Arriving back at the surgery, he was greeted by black looks and sarcastic remarks about locums and newly-fledged doctors in particular. The waiting room was filled to overflowing with the queue even extending some distance along the street.

Sandy was wet, cold and hungry, and had to attend to and listen to 40 sick, or near sick patients, dispense Heaven knows how many bottles of medicine and write out dozens of panel certificates and prescriptions before he could even start his visiting list. With a sinking feeling, he saw there were 38 people on it. He found himself thinking that being a doctor was not at all what it was cracked up to be. He wished heartily he was back in Paris with his painting and some peace.

He sighed ruefully; his mother had signally refused to stop badgering him that painting was 'no kind of a life to make a living from, so follow in your Father's footsteps.' So here he was in 1927 and newly-qualified, with two respectable degrees, Batchelor of Medicine and one in surgery; Alexander MacNeil M.B.Ch.B, in his thirties and physician and surgeon like his father. Now he was embarking on his first job in general practice, a locum in London's East End.

* * *

He saw the last patient out of the surgery and made his way back into the house in search of the domestic. He found her sitting in the kitchen with the morning paper.

'I say,' he said. 'Who's in charge of this outfit? I haven't even seen anyone yet.'

'Well sir,' she said, getting up hastily. 'Oh, I'm – I'm Lizzie sir. – I thought I could explain better when the patients 'ad gorn. Mrs. Clephane, the doctor's wife, told me to tell you when you'd finished to go up to The 'awthorns, – that's the name of their 'ouse, – and 'ave a talk with them there. They don't live 'ere y'see. They live in a posh 'ouse. This old 'ouse is just used as a surgery and the assistant lives 'ere.'

'Oh, there's an assistant is there?'

'No. There wuz. 'e got the sack and left larst week, couldn't get on with the missus or somethink, that's why you're 'ere. If the missus likes you, she may give you the job of assistant.'

'What about the doctor?' he asked. 'Has he no say in the matter?'

'Not much,' Lizzie said, looking glum. ''e's a very sick man and ill in bed and she's runnin' the practice.'

'She's qualified then? She's a doctor too?'

'Lord bless you! No sir! She's no doctor at all! But she's the boss awlright since the old doctor's took ill. 'e's a fine gentleman, the doctor, but Mrs. Clephane aint so easy. Bit difficult like – unless she takes a fancy to yer and then yer awlright – and there's no saying,' she added, looking him up and down and taking in his trim figure, hazel eyes and thick fair hair, 'that she might take a fancy to you, a smart fella like you.'

'Cut out the soap Lizzie. Where's this Hawthorns place?'

Sandy was a tad annoyed at this cavalier treatment but he learned later that cavalier was the usual way a locum, or assistant was treated. He was to find a future billet in

Hove where the doctor and family had already left and all the instructions, post and Patients' List were entrusted to the chauffeur. This obviously amused the chauffeur. Sandy was furious. Fat lot of respect for a qualified doctor he thought. He wasn't going to put up with that! He'd hand in his notice immediately. That he had then to inform the doctor through the chauffeur of his intention of resigning *and* within 24 hours, did not improve his impression of the attitude meted out to locums.

Following Lizzie's directions, he made his way up to the house.

Slightly surprised, he was received at the door by a butler. Hello, Sandy thought. Here they go one better than having an assistant!

The butler certainly looked the part. He was dignified, stoutish, clean-shaven with a bald dome and groomed side-burns. Sandy noted he had a decided twinkle in his eye. No doubt due to the effect of his employer's sherry, he thought, amused. He was shown into the lounge and announced in sonorous accents.

Standing in the middle of the room and graciously receiving him, was the doctor's wife. She affected a haughty air and had acquired a synthetic 'well-bred' accent. She was expensively dressed and gave Sandy the distinct impression that she hadn't completely recovered from 'being a doctor's wife.' He summed her up, he later found accurately, as a sales assistant from a West End shop. Mind you, a good class shop of the umpteen guinea gown type. Ever the cynic, and nicely honed through four years of war, he wondered how on earth she had nobbled the doctor.

It was already noon and she smelt aromatically of Gin and It. Would Sandy have a cocktail, she had just shaken one up? Sandy was quite agreeable! She was then careful to inform him as he sipped appreciatively at the excellent aperitif, that she did not believe in encouraging locums with alcohol, they were a drunken enough crowd as it was! She entertained him with descriptions of locums she had dealt with over the years in general practice 'and a drunken lot of irresponsible swine they were, I give you my word, but they met their Waterloo when they met me!' she said with a toss of her tawny head and grinned showing her white, but rather large teeth. She struck Sandy as too dangerous to cross.

She was, he guessed, about fifty and what was termed well-preserved. Rather above the average height for a woman, she was only a couple of inches short of his own height of 5ft. 11. With her pronounced high bosom, her heavy features with a roman nose and prominent blue eyes made bright and glistening from the gin she had been drinking, she was somewhat intimidating and to locums dependent on a job, doubly so, he thought.

'I hope you don't drink or fornicate,' she said helping herself to another cocktail. He blinked and murmured something about sitting down, he'd been drinking on an empty stomach, but she didn't appear to hear and paid this no attention. She stood up to her full height, her cocktail glass delicately poised and then gazed down at him with her intense blue eyes. He had an idea she was putting the 'fluence' on him.

'On one occasion,' she continued, 'I left in charge what I thought was a responsible locum while my husband and I took a holiday in the Austrian Tyrol. I always set my butler to watch and report on all our locums or assistants we employ, you know.' Thanks for the tip, thought Sandy and by now thinking rather longingly of food.

'The butler wrote that he wasn't completely satisfied,' she continued. 'The work was done alright but he suspected that the man drank and was making clandestine assignations with women.' Bully for him, thought Sandy, but where's the grub?

'Do you know, I worried myself sick for the rest of our month's stay! On our return, and only after the ruffian had left, I found stacks! literally stacks of empty bottles secreted in wardrobes and cupboards all over the house and evidence, very plain evidence that he had had women as bedmates on more than one occasion!'

Good for you chum! he thought, trying not to laugh. He agreed that the locum's behaviour was disgusting. 'I suppose the practice suffered?' he asked.

'Oh no!' admitted Mrs. Clephane. 'He did the work alright and everybody seemed charmed with him, especially the women, but it was his immoral behaviour I objected to. In any case I hounded that fellow from every Medical Agency in London and Manchester. I believe he made a cowardly escape by joining the West African Medical Service before I could catch him! I expect he's died of some frightful tropical disease by now,' she added somewhat regretfully, as a requiem to the supposed dead.

'He was so damned good-looking and a patient told me one of his girls looked like a well-known actress. She saw them driving in my car, *my* car, mind you! one fine Sunday afternoon in Hyde Park!' With that, she sat down in one of her large comfortable easy chairs and leaned back, gazing into space through half-closed lids, probably, Sandy thought, savouring her reminiscences of revenge.

He had a strong suspicion that her grievance against the luckless assistant was that he was so damned good looking and had dispensed his favours elsewhere.

'Well!' she said suddenly in a bright voice. 'Let us go in to lunch, I'm famished.' She rose sedately.

Lead me to it! rejoiced Sandy silently, getting up and hoping the food was worth the wait. She led the way.

'We'll go up and see the invalid afterwards. Oh yes. There's a surgery car, a small Austin for your use for house calls, – only when absolutely necessary you understand. The Daimler in the garage is for my use!' she added, as she swept into the dining room.

❧ Chapter 2 ❧

Sandy could not agree with Lizzie that the doctor lived in a posh house. The Hawthorns was certainly larger than the surgery house on the High Street and although there were no trams, buses from Battersea thundered down the road past it at regular intervals on their way to Putney and Wimbledon. He discovered later that situated on the main road, The Hawthorns' iron gate seemed to be the main stopping place for all the dogs in the neighbourhood, and the doctor's wife unsuccessfully endeavoured to sterilize it by daily deposits of chloride of lime. Diseases and dogs she disliked in equal measure. That the patients frequently brought their animals with them into the surgery waiting room horrified her. But that, she insisted, was to be only ever at the Surgery House.

The Hawthorns, from which those delightful trees had long since been cut down leaving an array of forlorn stumps plastered with soot, was he discovered, representative of hundreds of other doctors' houses all over England.

Here, a square of mouldy grass represented the lawn at the front of the house and there were two bay windows, two storeys and an attic. The ground floor held the dispensary, and the dining room he learned, was used as a waiting-room for private patients. The whole house was redolent of drugs, unguents and medicines. Also, that indefinable smell of the sick and unwashed who continually visited the surgery likewise pervaded this house, obviously from when they came up to the dispensary for their medicines and prescriptions; dogs to be left at the gate.

This smell naturally followed Sandy as he was escorted up to the patient's bedroom after lunch to meet Doctor Clephane at last.

He lay with his head partly swathed in bandages and as Sandy looked enquiringly at him, he muttered,

'Mastoiditis. It looks as if I'll be off for some time. I hope you are in no hurry away?'

Before Sandy could answer, he continued, 'Most of your work will be at the High Street surgery but I see some private patients here at this address. I mean, those that can afford a decent fee.' Obviously not wishing to sit with the panel patients, thought Sandy, irrepressibly. 'As you will be seeing those at 2 o'clock you will have lunch here daily but your other meals at the High Street and you'll sleep there as there are night calls.'

He was interested to discover Dr Clephane had an Ulster accent and thought he looked every bit an Irishman, with his big frame and thick hair and the keenest grey eyes. He had a large head with a wide mouth and a snub nose which gave him a boyish look despite his years.

'What on earth made you take up general practice?' he asked Sandy. 'It's a dog's life. – Look where it's landed me? – an old crock at 60, – all from serving an inconsiderate and ungrateful public. They may express sorrow at my death but they'll forget they killed me getting me out my warm bed on a cold night because they happen to have a bellyache,' he grunted, his Ulster accent making this more expressive. 'You'll learn that a favourite time for the phone to ring, is just when you've sat down to lunch. If you ask why they select this time they say 'that's the time we're sure to find you in.' And just try and have an evening off! When you're all set to go to the Theatre some old fool arrives to tell you that Gladys is in labour and 'sure as death I never knew she'd missed a period and gawd knows what the old man will say when he comes 'ome!' Oh, it's a great life if you don't weaken! Take my advice and become a Medical Officer of Health or join the L.C.C. You'll be no damned good to the community in either case but office hours and no night calls will make life more pleasant.'

This welcoming speech, half humourous and half bitter seemed to have exhausted Dr Clephane for his eyes closed wearily. Sandy could see how suddenly tired and worn he looked after this brief outburst. He wasn't quite sure what to make of it as he watched the Doctor fall asleep almost immediately.

Mrs. Clephane entered the room.

'Come along young man,' she greeted him, ushering him onto the landing. 'Surgery is downstairs at 2 you know and the nurse will be here shortly to attend to my husband. She's having her meal in the kitchen, much to her disgust. I hate nurses, silly upstarts,' she said sneeringly. 'A friend of mine summed them up properly. He said if a girl was too damned ugly to go into a shop and too stupid to be a shorthand typist, her people pushed her into the nursing profession! But why profession? Occupation I call it. I'm glad of the opportunity of showing this one her place by relegating her to the kitchen with the cook!'

Apart from bridling a little at being called 'young man,' Sandy wasn't going to take this. Curbing his instant annoyance, he ventured to disagree with her.

'My sister took up nursing because she felt it her vocation and she is a university graduate of distinction.'

'Oh well yes,' she answered dismissively, 'but how many do? About 1%, if that, I should say! Most of them have high hopes of snaffling a doctor as a husband, but I was glad to read somewhere that astonishingly few actually do!' Yes, thought Sandy, doctors got 'snaffled' by just about anybody if Mrs. Clephane was anything to go by.

By this time, he was feeling somewhat battered. First an event-filled morning almost at break-neck speed, followed by Mrs. Clephanes' oppressive welcome and then a nice little diatribe from the doctor of the practice. It was obvious however, that he was to stay. He'd passed muster with both Clephanes. He was gainfully employed. Thankfully, he did not now have to make an immediate return to that dismal waiting room at the Medical Agency in the Strand to wait in line for another job. Now he was to see the private patients before tackling those 38 calls on the visiting list. He devoutly hoped there would be an interval for food before facing evening surgery.

⌦ **Chapter 3** ⌫

Sandy speedily discovered that the majority of callers at a doctor's surgery did not need medical treatment at all. Numbers imagined they are ill, others needed nothing more than a brisk purge, as their poor diet was invariably augmented by stodgy foods or even consisted solely of such; little or no nutritional value; it just filled them up. Fish and chips and boiled eels might have their virtues but not as a staple diet. One patient said she'd been born constipated and another said with pride *she* was regular, 'every Sunday Doctor!' To combat such dyed-in-the wool beliefs was, he found, somewhat difficult.

Thus, the number of really sick people in need of immediate medical attention was very small indeed. But the numbers kept coming and needed dealing with.

He soon developed an acute observation and a sixth sense as soon as the patient was seated. With so many patients going through his hands at every surgery he had to keep his wits about him yet at the same time he also knew he couldn't afford to miss anything.

The panel system that had been devised was a mixed blessing. Whereas on one hand many individuals suffering from various illnesses would be unlikely or unable to consult a doctor at all, on the other, there was no doubt that many panel patients took undue advantage of their medical cards and kept the surgeries unnecessarily crowded. He discovered that every National Insurance practitioner was heartily sick of it as making the public 'surgery conscious' as so many made a habit of coming in for a panel certificate on a regular basis for the least thing. This gave the medicos an active dislike of the system.

Sandy was getting to know his regulars and discovered that they had been coming in from one years' end to the other on some pretext or another. As soon as one 'disease' cleared up they came in with another or for 'a bottle of tonic, Doctor.'

He actually had some sympathy for these wretched regulars. Although they were not essentially ill, they didn't feel well. The horrible food eaten by denizens of places like the Old Kent Road had to be seen to be believed. Foreign rabbit carcasses crawling with vermin and fancy foreign bread and cakes artificially coloured and tasting like sawdust, so-called 'cream buns' filled with some concoction one Belgian patient likened to paint – he who knew of genuine delicious Belgian pastries filled with real cream! Sandy seriously wondered if the Public Health Authority were even aware that the crude sackfuls of frozen Argentine meat designated for the poor was not cut up properly into joints but simply hacked into chunks and carelessly distributed to them, no doubt like that to all the big cities in the country.

Added to this, cleanliness and personal hygiene were largely unknown. As were the benefits he tried to draw to their attention. To many, these were either an anathema or unnecessary. As for fresh air, windows and doors were kept resolutely closed as a matter of course. Neither did their living conditions encompass or cater for any part of it. Amenities were derisory. They were inured to it.

But how to instill the idea that lack of hygiene and poor diet greatly undermined and even encouraged such conditions as the tuberculosis, pernicious anæmia and whole gamut of diseases that they were so used to was an enigma. They might listen to any words of well-intentioned advice but took no heed of them; to change their ingrained habits and mode of life was a Sysiphean task and asking too much.

Such nonchalance certainly tested his patience and even ingenuity in his attempts to get them to have some idea that they could help themselves to better health. However, those four years enduring and surviving the trenches seemed to Sandy to have been a perfect grounding for what he was confronting now, – positively tailor-made! he mused; the crowded intimacy, living with filth, lice, rats, and awful food. These had certainly taught him about people's endurance and extraordinary acceptance of horrible conditions alright. But that was war, Sandy sighed grimly. Here for so many it was a way of life.

Any illusions about being a doctor were assuming a dream-like quality. The East End of London was a far cry from his home town of Aberdeen and his father's discrete practice. This he had to admit had not been a significant part of his interest or education. He'd had no ambition in that direction and had left home as soon as possible. He'd gained his experiences in far different places.

He was certainly finding their value now as a doctor. For one, he was thankful he'd acquired a very broad view of life. Here he was right in at the deep end, no doubt of that! he thought. Thanks to the war especially, he had seen every aspect of human nature at its worst and best and every grade between. There could hardly be any surprises but doctoring meant a rather different impact, never mind approach. All eyes were on the doctor!

Though he rarely thought of those war years now he had learnt from them indelibly. They naturally coloured his biases and judgements and his cynicism had been nicely fostered; had indeed become a shield that one needed to acquire in order to live through it. Now he was glad of a measure of it for it gave him the professional detachment a doctor needed having to confront all manner of pain and suffering. How much easier it was being a seasoned man!

But the war had also left Sandy with a deep contempt for incompetence and waste, and judged it accordingly. Seeing the ghastly consequences at first hand surrounded by thousands of mangled bodies and decomposing corpses, tended to make one a little bitter. And there were always his own scattered scars and the piece of shrapnel still embedded in his lung as the occasional reminder.

He had however, definitely gained two over-riding priorities; plenty of sleep and good food! As a *locum tenens* filling in for established medical practitioners, he was to discover precious little of either.

* * *

Although not altogether good, he was fairly fortunate in the food at the Clephanes' though his sleep got regularly interrupted. He blessed his natural abounding good health and energy as he tackled his daily duties and rounds, though even for him it was frequently exhausting. No wonder old Clephane was feeling it at 60, he mused. Still, what else could the man do? He had to earn a living.

Sandy wasn't entirely happy at his introduction to general practice; three crowded surgeries a day, the intervals between packed with visits to patients' houses, the majority poor or sordid homes; all done on foot and at a great pace. Never mind the private patients, some requiring their pound of flesh. Then his sleep frequently disturbed as often as not by quite unnecessary night calls. This, with Lizzie the domestic's frying pan cookery, all combined to form a somewhat unattractive picture of his life as a locum. He felt that at this rate he was going to age rather rapidly.

He didn't take to that idea! He had a certain amount of pride in looking much younger than his years. He needed to! Dash it, in three years he'd be 40! He laughed at his own conceit and put his faith in the hardy fibre of his Highland ancestry and his humourous view of life and people.

After he had evolved some kind of a routine however, he began gradually to look forward to the crowded surgeries and even visits, for as well as his expanding knowledge in actually practicing medicine, he was getting an intimate insight into the actual lives of the working and poorer classes. Poor circumscribed lives, rarely enlivened by interesting happenings they made birth, marriage and death the key points of their existence, especially death.

And birth and death naturally closely involved the local doctor.

A death was an event more solemn, more thrilling, and certainly more expensive, than any other. This was readily understood by anyone who witnessed an East End of London funeral. These barbaric obsequies were a tremendous source of revenue to the undertakers of London. Nearly every cockney would have contributed a few coppers a week to some Friendly Society in order to ensure that at death their funeral would be in a style that their relatives' prestige would not be lowered, indeed, even enhanced. This money was never used for anything other than the funeral of the donor.

Sandy found that families got into such a frenzy of spending on these occasions in order to out-vie some neighbours' funeral that they exceeded the insurance payments and got into debt to the mortician.

His patients' conditions and idiosyncrasies certainly enlivened life. Through practicing medicine in this teaming part of the East End and confronting peoples' lives at such an intimate level he was enlarging his observations and experiences at a great rate. Caught up so thoroughly in this fresh view of everything, Sandy's curiosity in the odd, the extraordinary, the unorthodox and challenging was thus being well satisfied. With his increasing medical proficiencies too, regardless of exhaustion, he found life full of interest and certainly rich in that unpredictability he liked.

But there was one thing he never got used to. The street accident. He wasn't alone in this in the profession he discovered; he later met a surgeon who would run, literally run from a street accident. Why should this be when as doctors they see much blood and tears? Why should a wrecked car at a badly-lit crossroads on a rainy night with broken glass littering the road, blood oozing out from under the door jammed shut, with not a sound, not even a moan from inside, make even a hardened doctor approach the scene with a sick feeling in his stomach? Well, it did Sandy.

Of course, there were often accidents in the home and an urgent call out for the doctor, ergo, Sandy. One night at 11 o'clock just as he was going to bed an urgent call had him hurrying to an address in a dark side street in Garret Green. A Mrs. Lugg had heard a thump and groans coming from her next-door neighbour's house. Rushing round and into the house she'd found Mrs. McGann lying on the floor and groaning in pain. The locum was sent for.

Met at the door by the concerned Mrs. Lugg holding a guttering candle, Sandy was led through a narrow doorway into a low-ceilinged, grubby and poorly furnished room. On the far side huddled at the foot of a stairway lay Mrs. McGann.

He hastened across the room with Mrs Lugg and her candle but there was no room to examine the poor woman. Failing to lift her, Mrs. Lugg lent her aid but in vain; Mrs. McGann was at least 20 stone, so together they dragged her as carefully as possible across the filthy floor and onto a very dirty old rug in front of the fireless grate. By the light of the candle Sandy could see the lady was seriously injured.

Suddenly the door opened and a stoker in naval ratings uniform stood, swaying drunkenly. 'Wot's goin' on 'ere?'

he growled, blinking owlishly and peering at the trio by the fireplace.

'This is the Doctor,' snapped Mrs. Lugg. 'Yer ole woman 'as fallen an 'urt 'erself.'

'Christ!' howled the sailor. 'The bloody ole woman's fallen dahnstairs!' He started to blubber noisily. 'It's all my bleedin' fault. S'pose she wondered why I was so late an' tried to get dahn 'erself. C'mon Doc, gives a han' to git 'er up to 'er bunk.'

Sandy suggested the hospital and got a blank refusal. He was a powerfully built man, and before Sandy could say anything further, stooped, and proceeded to hoist the unconscious bulk of his mother to her feet, her head lolling on his shoulder. Sandy then saw in the dim uncertain light of the candle, that they had another visitor. A blonde-haired young woman had been concealing herself behind the sailor's broad back. She had a fatuous grin on her face and looked as if she had been imbibing a fair quantity of alcohol.

'Never mind 'er Doc. That's my bint, my blonde. It's 'er bleedin' fault I'm late!'

'Garn,' she replied. 'It's yer own. Yer wouldn't wait till we got 'ome, yer 'ad to drag me up the alleyway!'

'Shut up you,' the sailor bawled, 'and gives a 'and to git the old woman on me back.'

This was an extraordinary performance but jointly they managed it somehow and the procession started upstairs, the sailor leading the way with his mother's body collapsed heavily on his back, her arms hanging over his shoulders, and her feet trailing on the stairs. The rest of them tried to support the inert figure and with many grunts and curses from the sailor and giggles from his blonde, they squeezed up the filthy stairway. As a result of the combined pressure the old woman began to pass wind noisily to the great amusement of the half-drunk young woman.

By the time they got the poor creature on the bed, she had expired.

It took some time for the stoker to grasp that his dear mother was dead and when he did, he sat down beside her on the untidy bed and howled in earnest, upbraiding his sweetheart in no uncertain terms.

Since Sandy could do no more, he felt it was high time to leave. He went downstairs followed by Mrs. Lugg. She detained him by the door with a touch on his arm. 'You'll be Dr Clephane's locum? – Never mind sir! Before you've been 'ere long, yer'll get used to it!' With that the frowsy old dame grinned, showing a fine set of tartar-covered teeth, and darted into her house.

He walked along the deserted street inhaling draughts of what passed for fresh air in Garret Green in an attempt to clear his nose of the smells and his mind of the scene he had just witnessed. He walked rapidly and reflected that if a nice big coffin could be found no doubt the funeral would be a splendid one.

⚓ Chapter 4 ⚓

In general practice there were frequent emergency calls with the formula – 'Doctor! Come at once!' – but Sandy found that a real emergency was luckily surprisingly rare.

He was still new to the practice and a very real emergency came in the middle of a busy surgery; Doctor come at once, a child was in convulsions. Seizing his bag, he set off quickly on foot as the house was only a step away, urgently turning over in his mind all the causes and treatments he could think of.

On arrival, he was met by the anxious parents and taken up to the child they said was a little boy, just 6 years old. There Sandy found him shuddering on the bed, in a state called *status epilepticus*, wracked with convulsion after convulsion at short intervals with no return to consciousness. The poor little patient was covered in sweat and pale with exhaustion.

Sandy was greatly perturbed and did his best to hide it from the parents – he knew of it but had not seen it before – as he racked his brains as to what to give him. He was too young for morphia and chloral and bromide p.r. was impractical so rapidly dismissed. Then he made a decision and dived into his bag for chloroform and a mask. Gently anæsthetizing the boy, the convulsions gradually ceased and the little body relaxed and he breathed naturally and easily. He was now in a calm sleep and cooler to the touch. Sandy though, was not breathing easily, he was agitated and not daring to show it. Had he done the right thing? He barely heard the parents' praise and thanks.

'When Timmy had an attack a year ago,' they then said, 'the doctor simply did not know what to do and let him convulse it out, with the poor child nearly dying in the process!'

With some misgiving Sandy assured them that all would be well.

He hurried back to the surgery to ring up Dr Clephane, who was now well enough to sit out in a chair, and asked his opinion.

'Good Lord!' he exclaimed in some irritation. 'You had a nerve! You and your chloroform! You Scotchmen think the stuff is a talisman for everything! Why in thunder didn't you give him an eighth of a grain of morphine or paraldehyde p.r.! It'll be a miracle if the bairn is alive in the morning.'

But the bairn was alive and well in the morning and all the succeeding mornings that he saw him. As long as he remained in Garret Green the boy never had another fit and the parents saw to it that Sandy got his mead of praise.

Then one evening, he had a call at the surgery that was to bring something to his notice that he was only vaguely aware of.

He had thankfully closed and bolted the surgery door when an insistent knocking compelled him to re-open it. A pale and agitated woman stood there and asked anxiously if she could see him for a few moments. Naturally Sandy invited her in and she immediately explained that it was about her son. She didn't want him necessarily to come to see him that night but just give her something or a prescription as the boy was in pain. This was in his back and he couldn't sleep because of it.

He was feeling pretty tired by now so didn't enquire further into the symptoms but gave the woman some aspirin and a belladonna plaster saying he would call on the morrow. She seemed satisfied with this and left.

He gave it no more thought until out on his rounds. Finding the house, he rang the bell. The door was answered not by the mother but by a woman with a distinct family resemblance so he thought probably her sister.

'Ronnie's mother is out,' she explained, 'but I'll take you up.'

Sandy found Ronnie in his pyjamas and lying face down on the bed. He was an attractive boy with wavy fair hair and smooth clear skin.

'Your treatment didn't help much Doctor,' he said with a charming but self-conscious smile.

'Sorry,' said Sandy, smiling back. 'Let's have a look,' and turned up the back of his jacket to palpate his back.

'No sir, it isn't there. The pain is right down on my tail-bone. I can't sit or lie on my back without it hurting.'

On examination Sandy found a small inflamed area and the coccyx displaced or even fractured, he thought.

'How did you get this? Did someone kick you?'

'No sir.'

'Did you have a fall then?'

'No sir.'

'Alright, don't worry,' Sandy said. 'I'll do a little gentle manipulation now and send you some suppositories.'

As he left the boy's room, he found the aunt waiting for him outside.

Heading for the stairs she said, 'May I talk to you confidentially?'

'What about?' he asked, puzzled at the odd tone in her voice.

'About Ronnie. Haven't you any idea of what has been happening to that boy Doctor? Or must I explain?'

'I admit, I am rather mystified by how he came by that injury,' he answered. 'He won't give me any clue.'

'And small wonder,' she replied tightly. 'But I know. His mother won't admit to it even to herself, but as a woman of the world and one who has lived abroad, she must know and ought to! Come downstairs and I'll tell you the whole story and you can judge for yourself.'

He followed obediently and they went into the lounge.

'About a year ago,' the woman began, 'my sister took Ronnie out of school – he wasn't very good at his lessons, but the Astoria, you know, that Hotel in the West End? took him on as a page – on account of his looks I suppose. A few months ago, he started wearing the most beautifully cut clothes and expensive shoes and seemed to have plenty of money for the pictures and the like. He told his mother quite candidly, that there was a very wealthy and titled gentleman who had a permanent suite at the Astoria who took a great interest in him. He liked to take the boy out on his off-duty, – took him to Art galleries, museums, music concerts at Queens' Hall, that sort of thing and seemed keen on improving the boy's mind. My sister was very impressed with all this and flattered by it. But I wasn't, I assure you, I tell you straight! 'I've heard of men like him before,' I said! 'Don't you remember the trial of Oscar Wilde? – If the man was so interested in Ronnie, why didn't he come and see you, his mother?' Well, she kept promising to invite him round but in her usual off-handed way kept putting it off – or making excuses that we weren't grand enough for titled gentlemen! She said I had an evil mind and she saw no harm in the association. Now, Doctor, – what conclusion would you have come to?'

Sandy was appalled at the imputation in the aunt's story but had to admit to himself that her suspicions seemed reasonably correct. Immediately he was overcome with the embarrassment usually felt by the British male towards anything morally unpleasant.

Chiding himself for being cowardly, he side-stepped it and said, 'Well, I think I had better see his mother tomorrow and have a talk with her about it.'

He left the house determined to ask Dr Clephane's advice on how he should deal with this.

The following day, he found an opportunity to speak to Dr Clephane and related what the aunt had told him. He was uncompromising in his reply.

'Don't have anything to do with it,' he said. 'Let them work it out themselves. All you have to do as their medical advisor is to treat the boy's physical disability and leave his morals to the parents or the parson. The parson may know more about homosexuality than you do. I don't mean to be unnecessarily cynical but my experience is that interference or ill-timed advice in a case like this will only recoil on your own head.'

'But haven't we any kind of responsibility?' asked Sandy. 'He's well under age, barely sixteen I'd say and…'

'Listen young crusader, just after the South African War, I was foolish enough to tell a woman patient that she had been infected with venereal disease. That remark nearly cost me my life! I had her large soldier husband, who had doubtless infected her, burst into my house with a loaded revolver, threatening me with a violent death if I did not recant! This was before the days when you sent such cases to clinics whose diagnosis cannot be questioned and who take any onus for naming the disease. I was only too happy to recant and I've never named the disease to a patient since. If a patient contracts VD, I just treat it, that's all. I've no interest in how or from whom. I know some medical men set themselves up as a court of morals and give free advice to patients about their domestic life and behaviour. I've never found that a paying proposition. Mind your own business is an excellent motto for the profession.'

Sandy felt there was something wrong with the doctor's argument. All kinds of villainy which might be exposed by the better-informed profession would go unchecked. But he was to learn that authority, the law and even the public were not interested in the profession's ideas on unusual divergencies of behaviour. A judge in a case of an offender against public morals was not interested in any pathological reasons offered by the defence.

'The accused has broken the law and I am here to administer the law,' was his dictum. The man was duly sentenced.

Bearing Dr Clephane's advice in mind and because the boy himself had given him no clue at the time, when Ronnie's mother came to see him at the surgery, he regretted that he could form no opinion as to how the boy had come by his injury. Concealing his qualms, he could only add that it was his belief that a change of occupation was indicated. He felt it was the best he could do.

In any case, Sandy found that the patients did not come for advice. If occasionally it was proffered regards elementary hygiene and diet to improve the ailment, they'd listen patiently and then simply demand a bottle of medicine. This is where their interest and faith lay. If that was not forthcoming from the panel doctor, they turned to patent medicines. The medicine was to fix it. It seemed to Sandy, that they still had some mediæval notion that there was some marvelous elixir that would cure all ills. He even found among the private patients whose only need was for less of the 'stalled ox' and more of the 'dish of herbs' to reduce their obesity to improve their health, that they too wanted their talisman, 'a bottle of tonic Doctor.'

⏵ Chapter 5 ⏴

Slowly and surely Dr Clephane began to improve due to the combined skills of the specialist who attended him and the nurse Mrs. Clephane had relegated to the kitchen for meals. He got more cheerful and expansive and liked Sandy's company when he could stay after lunch.

He found in Sandy someone whose varied life's experiences and now a certain maturity made their conversations interesting and stimulating. New to the profession yes, but he had things to talk about outside of Clephane's own life. Also, rather a novelty from the mostly medical exchanges with those who came to the practice.

In turn he entertained Sandy with tales of his life in Ireland and his early struggles, as well as much good advice on how to be a successful practitioner. This suited Sandy very well as he liked the man's acerbic wit and colourful prose drily delivered in his deep Ulster voice.

He admitted to indulging in a little hocus pocus when building up his practice. Accordingly, he stuck a thermometer into the mouth of every patient and made professional play with his stethoscope, listening to the patient's chest if the slightest occasion warranted it. This gave him the reputation of painstaking thoroughness, while the use of the ophthalmoscope with its little refracted light shone into the eye was a source of wonder in Garret Green.

He amused Sandy by admitting that no matter if the patient had a broken leg, he had his temperature taken and his heart ausculated and a bottle of tonic prescribed. In time the good doctor was so busy that he had no time for all these attentions unless actually necessary.

By this time the doctor asked him to call him Patrick when they were together. He went on to tell Sandy how he'd qualified in Glasgow in the 1890's and after doing a short assistantship there moved to fresh fields in London. A fellow Irishman had written of a likely spot to put up his plate which turned out to be Garret Green.

Duly arrived, he toured the whole area on his bicycle and deemed the growing suburb had good possibilities. He found an agreeable landlady and with a few pounds, his bike and a new brass plate, he was launched. Patience, hard work and his natural Irish charm brought him his patients alright. As the suburb grew so did his practice. He had a natural flair for midwifery too. Just with his large frame and easy Irish charm Sandy felt sure he made a vitally reassuring presence at these important and intimate events and impressed Sandy with 3000 confinements to his credit. He felt this alone justified Dr Clephane's existence.

But how easy it was to come under criticism, no matter of an experienced doctor, he learned one day after leaving the house after lunch.

An elderly man came along as he was about to get into the surgery car and begged a lift to the High Street. He soon realized that the man had lain in wait for him to vent his criticism of Dr Clephane to his new and relatively untried locum.

Sandy was annoyed but the traffic was heavy so he was stuck with this disgruntled patient and unable to stop the man's flow of complaint. He said how the doctor had been attending him for severe gastric pain for years and treating him with diet and alkalis. But despite the doctor's treatment, he said derisorily, the pain got worse and he was losing weight and pale as a sheet. From the man's description Sandy surmised Dr Clephane had palpated the man's abdomen at this stage. On discovering a hard mass at the site of the old ulcer, the doctor had diagnosed this as a neo-plasm; a cancerous tumour. He told the man's wife of this diagnosis and she promptly passed this alarming news to her husband which frightened the pair of them considerably.

The upshot was that he consulted someone else and eventually after X-rays and recommended exploratory surgery at the hospital, instead of a tumour, a thick hardened mass was found to have developed over successfully healed ulcers, simulating a growth. This was dealt with and the man made an excellent recovery but he was furious with Dr Clephane for this mis-diagnosis, frightening his wife and himself un-necessarily and said he had no business to have got it wrong. And, he finished in a pleased voice, he hadn't spoken to the doctor since.

While he understood the man's anger, Sandy was still annoyed at this petty revenge by waylaying his locum to miscall him and his dismissal of the man who had given him years of attention and that all his qualities as a good doctor were cast aside.

Glad at last to let the patient, jubilant at scoring over a doctor, out at the High Street, Sandy was then thrown a Parthian shot. 'Take the advice of one who knows Doc. Don't diagnose cancer off your own bat!'

Sandy resolved never to do so.

But the more he saw of Dr Clephane the more he liked and respected him. He was getting restive by now so began to assist him in what Sandy felt were his more difficult cases. But, he realized, difficult to a beginner.

One night attending a confinement, he realized this was going to be a breach birth; instead of the head of the infant presenting itself to the world, the other end was about to appear. Could he deal successfully with the limbs and then deliver the aftercoming head properly? All the possible disasters crowded his mind.

He phoned Dr Clephane voicing his misgivings. He arrived grinning all over his face and filling Sandy with confidence as he greeted the mother and sat down joining Sandy who had returned to the presenting breach. To Sandy's surprise, he made no effort to interfere and delivered the babe intact just as if it had been a normal head presentation.

'Midwifery, or 'Howdie' as you call it in Scotland,' Dr Clephane said as they left, 'is all a matter of common sense plus experience. If you keep your text book in front of you, you'll just get the wind-up. Leave it to nature, but if nature fails, and she very rarely does, only then are you justified in interfering. The point is to recognize when and if nature is failing and that comes with experience. Another fault of you chaps is putting on the forceps too early. You get impatient perhaps or the midwife wants to get home to her bed, senses you are a green hand and subtly suggests 'the tongs' – fight shy of this type of midwife. You'll find, like nurses, good midwives are born not made. And Irish ones are the best,' he finished, sententiously.

'Beats me,' Sandy remarked, 'why babies so frequently choose to arrive either when they are not expected or in the middle of the night.'

'That's a daft question laddie,' replied the doctor with a grin. 'Let's get to our beds!'

Dr Clephane was not a brilliant doctor but he was conscientious and not afraid of work. He had made a considerable fortune but sadly took no real pleasure in it. He had no interests in the arts, music or real literature and no hobbies to spend it on so was easily bored and restless when not working.

Thus, he was glad of Sandy's company. Since his wife was frequently out dining, dancing, theatre or cinema, Sandy occasionally had his evening meal with him. He didn't resent his wife's absences but he was noticeably restless and paced about the lounge falling into reminiscences of his boyhood in Armagh.

He was patently an unhappy man and used Irish whiskey and food to console himself, feeling and concluding that his advancing years were inhibiting his activities. A naturally robust man he was now fed up. His one interest, golf, he'd had to give up due to arthritic knees. The result was that he'd since grown heavier and bulkier and fatter and ever more disgruntled with himself.

Bridget, his wife, said it took all her patience to live with and amuse him. But the only amusement Sandy ever saw her provide was a weekly bundle of 'thrillers.'

One day he had a surprise visit from the butler with a written invitation to 'dine at The Hawthorns.' It was signed by Bridget, not, he noted by 'Mrs Clephane.'

Why this honour, he thought. She was rarely at the lunchtime meals and out on most evenings so presuming she would be at the dinner he was interested to take further stock of her. She was rather an unknown quantity and he was ever curious about people.

He was always glad to escape from Lizzie's less than imaginative culinary efforts at the evening meal. He could not in honesty class these meals as 'dinner,' everything being cooked as always, in a frying pan and frequently over-cooked. He doubted their nutritional value and devoutly hoped his digestive tract would survive the onslaught during his locum stint.

Having lunched at the Hawthorns and enjoyed the food there, he had high hopes of this more formal meal with the Clephanes, so set off with anticipation.

He was shown into the lounge where Dr Clephane politely but very slowly rose to greet him.

'Take a seat me boy. James the butler ye know, will bring you some of those cocktail things in a minute. His name isn't James at all. It's plain Clancy, but Bridget insists on calling him James. She thinks it's more refined, ye see.'

He subsided into his chair and took a satisfying swallow from a cut glass tumbler on the table beside him. It was plain to Sandy that from his pronounced accent and beaming countenance, the doctor had been imbibing considerable amounts of his favourite poteen already.

Always careful of his appearance, Sandy had dressed with care.

'That's a fine suit you're wearing laddie! Where did you get it?'

'Miller's, Hanover Square,' he replied. 'My father's tailor. He always held that good clothes always impress so it pays to be well-dressed. Your own suit Doctor, strikes me as pretty good incidentally.'

'It ought to be,' he growled looking up from his tumbler. 'Some damned Dutchman made it in Saville Row, naturally to Bridget's specifications and knocked me back some twenty guineas. In Armagh I could have got ten suits for that dammit! She says the Dutchman makes suits for Royalty if that's a recommendation!'

At that moment, Clancy, or rather James, entered with the cocktails and indicated his tray.

'Dry martini Sir or Side Car?' he asked Sandy. He chose a Martini.

'Bridget likes a Side Car,' said Dr Clephane. 'She's dolling herself up no end for you laddie, so beware! Clancy, get me another whiskey and mix up a dozen of these Side Car things. We're thirsty.'

As James left, Bridget made her entrance and Sandy heard her mutter 'and make 'em strong,' as she passed him.

She sailed forward, hand outstretched in greeting.

'Delighted you've come Doctor. Finish your drink and have another,' she said flashing him a smile and consequently those rather large teeth.

They kept on 'having another' as Bridget paraded around in a magnificent evening dress of ivory satin, with pearls in her tawny hair and talking nineteen to the dozen. She made Sandy think of Lucretia Borgia, for some reason. She certainly looked an impressive figure with her high colour, roman nose and her large blue eyes flashing as she talked. This was mainly of personalities and criticisms of all and sundry. He found all this deeply uninteresting and kept thinking of the hollowness of his interior and when was dinner going to materialize.

Meanwhile Dr Clephane had got to the stage of just sitting and beaming alcoholically. Sandy sat in a sort of fog himself watching Bridget's performance and vaguely wondering at this glimpse of the married life of a medical man.

Bridget's inhibitions were obviously loosening up from her steady consumption of Side Cars as she giggled girlishly and asked, 'Have you heard the one about the French girl who preferred it cold?' whereby Dr Clephane stirred himself sufficiently to growl, 'Cut that out Bridget and let's get some food.'

'Half a tick! I want to show the locum some of my things. The way he's looking at my frock I'd say he'd like to see some of them,' she said, bending her blue eyes on to Sandy, and promptly flew from the room. To his astonishment she then began to dash up and down stairs with great speed and enthusiasm bearing various frocks, short coats, mink things, sequin-studded evening dresses, silk pyamas and the like.

He made what he could of it all feeling very much as if he was in some West End showroom as she proceeded to drape every available piece of furniture in the lounge with these exotic garments.

The Doctor sat looking apologetically at Sandy while he in fact, after his first astonishment was quietly enjoying this extraordinary performance. This was totally new in his experience.

She was still downing her Side Cars as her enthusiasm increased about her wardrobe but then as she dashed upstairs promising even more delights she failed to return and the sound of retching could be heard from the bathroom. The violent exercise and all the excitement were patently too much for her.

'You see,' said Dr Clephane, staring gloomily into his glass, 'that's what Bridget does and it invariably ends in a puking match. If she'd married earlier and had a child...' He took another swig. 'We've only been married five years y'see and she's now coming up to 50. I was late to the married state as I had a disappointing love affair when I was a young man. The girl married someone else and went out to Malaya where she died poor thing and I never dreamt of marrying. Five years ago, I started the otitis which ended in this mastoid. I was lying sick here under the doubtful care of a housekeeper when Bridget's father, a long-term friend and patient of mine called to see me. In no time, Bridget and her mother had ousted the housekeeper and taken over the nursing of me. I suppose out of gratitude, or loneliness or something, I married the daughter.' He grew suddenly silent as he heard his wife descending the stairs.

She re-appeared looking a trifle *distrait* and haggard but otherwise composed. She made no reference to the incident but announced that the meal would be ready any minute. It seemed she had signalled the butler as he appeared almost at once to say that dinner was served.

It was a good meal and Sandy and the doctor did it full justice. Bridget did not seem particularly hungry. A Veuve Clicquôt was served with the food which she and Sandy drank but Dr Clephane stuck to his poteen. The meal finished, after coffee and a cigar he made his excuses and left.

In spite of the odder aspects of the evening he had enjoyed himself. This was the first time he'd actually spent time with them together; invariably he'd met them singly, seen them as individuals, so this was his first experience of a medical man's domestic and private life. This was not as dignified and austere as would appear to the outsider. They were patently quite human and prone to all the foibles and weaknesses of ordinary people after all.

◗ **Chapter 6** ◖

Dr Clephane was a generous man like most of his compatriots. His wife had carte blanche for her clothing and pleasures which she took full advantage of.

One Saturday evening, Sandy went over to join Dr Clephane after dinner at his request as his wife was going out. As Bridget went upstairs, ostensibly to fix her face, he asked Sandy if he'd do him a favour and take his wife out to whatever entertainment she fancied; he would foot the bill.

He agreed, foreseeing a pleasant evening. Although he sometimes joined the doctor when his wife was out gallivanting, he was usually bored after evening surgery, either reading or going to the pictures and this promised to be an interesting change.

Bridget was full of zeal at this suggestion. They took the Daimler and to Sandy's delight not only was he to drive the luxurious car but she said they should head for the Café de Paris.

The Café was crowded but she seemed quite *au fait* with the place and impressed him by securing a table with no trouble at all. They made a pretence at ordering a meal with two bottles of what she called 'bubbly.' She pushed aside her omelette and settled down to frequent replenishment of her glass. The choice of liquor was absolutely in line with Sandy's as this wine was of the finest.

They got up to dance and as this was a favourite of his, the Charleston, he gave of his spirited best. Then he caught sight of Bridget's very well-fleshed posterior in a mirror shaking vigorously to the rhythm of the dance. This was both alarming and off-putting. But despite these substantial hips she was very light on her feet so avoiding any glances at the mirror he was able to enjoy dancing with her. Full of enthusiasm and bubbly, she matched Sandy dance for dance.

What with the wine, the sophisticated Café de Paris and the dancing, Bridget was enjoying herself hugely. When they returned to the table after a well-executed fox-trot, she leaned forward, face flushed and flashed a happy and toothy smile at Sandy.

'You know Sandy MacNeil, you are very handsome with your lovely fair hair and pretty eyes. I bet lots of women fall for you?'

'Oh! er, too busy these days,' he mumbled, then hoped that this didn't offer any sort of encouragement.

He'd had plenty of fun and games of course throughout his adult life but this was quite new, getting the come on from a woman considerably older than himself. Thanks to the wine this was a trifle flattering but as those blue eyes gazed somewhat glassily into his he started to feel a trifle panicky and so suggested they dance again. Distraction was definitely the best and immediate option.

In due course, Bridget decided a move was in order. 'Let's call it a day Sandy. I'm tired.'

He guessed that fatigue and her age were telling on her at last despite the artificial stimulus of the wine and the dancing.

As he drove out of Moon's garage, she remarked that it was a lovely night and why not go out to the Kingston By-pass and park somewhere. He drove out that way but was extremely dubious about the 'parking somewhere.' As the car rolled swiftly on, she leant nearer and rested her tawny head on his shoulder.

'Careful,' warned Sandy discouragingly. 'We might be seen.'

'Who cares,' she gurgled happily. 'I haven't had so much fun since the bed fell on Father! I warn you Sandy dear, before the night's out I'm going to make love to you, or you will make love to me!'

Suddenly she sat up and cried indignantly, 'Have you any idea what a woman of my temperament can suffer, tied to a man who is impotent? I admit that Clephane is one of the best and there isn't a thing I wouldn't do to make him comfortable but there is more to married life than merely looking after the creature comforts of your spouse! What I have suffered! Why, it's five years since I enjoyed the kiss of a normal passionate man!'

Not a conversational gambit he was willing to pursue, Sandy didn't answer but drove on and as she went on to moan about the lack of passion in her life in its several ramifications, he hoped she'd soon run out of steam.

Peeved that he was so unresponsive, she turned towards him and said sulkily,

'Be human Sandy and make love to me or I'll tell Clephane.'

'Tell him what?' he said nervously, trying to keep his eye on his driving.

'I'll tell him you tried to seduce me and that I repulsed you!'

Well, complaint or not Sandy wasn't going to lay a finger on her. He determined that come what may he would keep her attention off the subject as she lolled back in her seat, well under the influence and probably enjoying in anticipation the result of her cunning.

As a consequence, he kept up a sort of gentle running commentary on the view, the stars, anything trivial that came to mind and stepped discretely on the gas. He kept up as much speed as the built-up area would permit, heartily glad that the beautiful car was such a smooth ride that she seemed to be relaxed and drowsy. So smooth was the ride that Bridget was back in her own garage before she knew where she was.

'You little swine!' she spluttered. 'We're home!' her eyes popping more than ever with astonishment and chagrin.

The old doctor had heard the car and was standing at the door smiling expansively; he had obviously been solacing himself with whiskey.

'Enjoyed yourselves, have you? You're home rather early?'

Bridget pushed roughly past him and made a bolt for the stairs. Clephane led the way into the lounge, assuming Sandy was following. He poured him a beer and himself another Irish.

'Well sir,' he said lamely. 'Mrs. Clephane didn't care too much about coming home early but I have lot of visits in the morning and I like my sleep.'

'Don't worry me boy. I know her trouble. You didn't come up to scratch. You aren't the first good-looking locum I've had. Also there have been a few assistants; some have, – but some haven't come up to scratch either, – but they all left eventually. You see I can take all this sort of thing in my stride. As a medical man I can understand physical urges and the lambent flame in a woman flaring in late middle age. Not that I advocate promiscuity, but you know how it can be, the woman, the time, the place and the opportunity.' He looked glumly into his glass and took another consoling swallow.

It was a relief to Sandy to know he was fully aware of his wife's propensities. Bridget swept into the room on a cloud of Chanel and sat down beside her husband and patted his hand. Sandy was treated to a diabolical smile and a hard stare from her which augered no good for him. He felt it would be a good idea to contrive an escape from this locum soon as he did not relish any more approaches from Bridget. Pity, he liked old Clephane.

* * *

His locum in fact finished rather sooner than planned. Sandy came down with acute bronchitis and spent a miserable two days in bed. Bridget had her revenge by proclaiming several times a day that she wasn't going to have any invalids around, she had invalids enough. Doctor Clephane said he was fit to resume work fully now so asked Sandy if he would mind going. Nothing would suit him better, he thought.

On the night before his departure, Bridget took herself off and he and Sandy sat together after dinner, a bottle of whiskey between them. Clephane then opened his heart to him.

He was afraid of this noisy barbarous woman who had nailed him to the matrimonial mast, he said. He was afraid of her vitality, her voice, her colossal brass neck, her monopolizing of him and his home. In fact, her whole make-up. He had imagined that wives were sweet, charming companions and comforters as his mother had been. This new 'modern woman' was more than he could cope with.

With several large measures of neat whiskey inside him his Irishness increased.

'It's an abstruse and complicated sociological problem,' he said solemnly, gazing at Sandy rather mournfully. 'But she's a product of the age,' he muttered. 'A strong-minded robust female determined not to go under as so many of her sex do, with no intellectual or other qualifications. Her only means of attaining any security was by the exercise of her cunning, iron will and self-confidence to ensnare a man of position and money, and by God, she succeeded! But it's tough on an old man Sandy. Tough!'

The following day he left the Doctor with a certain amount of regret; Clephane was a good man. He felt he'd been fortunate in him as a mentor, and his first locum had been pretty good on the whole; he'd learnt a great deal. Also, the East End had been a perfect place for encountering a wide variety of infections and diseases and even much dealing with the effects of strife among such crowded humanity. He'd certainly learned his midwifery skills from the best and much worldly medical advice besides. Sandy wanted badly to know how the old doctor fared.

It was many months later that Sandy learned sad news of him. He'd kept in touch with one of his patients who lived close by so he heard the whole harrowing tale.

One night, this neighbour found the poor doctor actually outside his house, in the street, delirious and in his pyjamas, the trousers slipped down past his knees. These had tripped him up. The neighbour had gently taken his old and rambling friend indoors again, past the frightened servants and got him into his bed. He'd gone rapidly into a coma. The neighbour asked the butler where Mrs. Clephane was to be found. He answered in a scared way that she was out with the new locum, an Egyptian gentleman.

The kind friend had sent immediately for another doctor but before a colleague arrived poor old Clephane from Armagh had expired.

The funeral was splendid, his correspondent George told him. Hundreds followed the coffin, especially those who owed him money and the Widow's weeds were of the finest. She was leaning for consolation on the arm of the Egyptian locum. George added 'drunkenly' and other derogatory remarks which included the new locum which made Sandy chuckle and rather wished he'd been there himself.

▪ Chapter 7 ◂

Sandy meanwhile had been sent by the Agency to a semi-fashionable resort on the Thames Estuary; a locum was needed to assist for a period an aged practitioner, a Scot like himself, Dr Grant.

After an hour's journey from Fenchurch Street Station, he was met at his destination by the doctor. He didn't make an impressive sight Sandy thought. He was thin with a tired and seedy look. His motor car was an ancient tourer which heightened the impression of indigence somewhat. After a curt greeting, he merely signed to Sandy to get into the old tourer. His heart sank; this billet didn't indicate any home comforts.

The doctor's old car trundled along at barely 20 miles an hour and eventually pulled up in a side street off the main London Road, which Sandy discovered later, led to the sea. The house they'd arrived at was an unobtrusive but substantial two-storied villa fronted by a mildewed wooden paling. Unimpressed by this sign of neglect he then saw on the rickety wooden gate the smallest brass plate he had ever imagined on a doctor's house.

Once inside the house, Dr Grant motioned Sandy to an armchair in his comfortable though over-furnished sitting room, which he called the parlour. Tea was brought by a neatly dressed woman whom he introduced as his housekeeper. Sandy thought perhaps this was a reasonable billet after all.

Dr Grant gazed quizzically at his locum from under his beetling grey eyebrows. Then to Sandy's relief started to make conversation and informed him that his duties would be light and daily visits would be few as there was no panel and only a limited number of private patients. That sounded good to Sandy.

As they drank their tea the doctor unwound a little and revealed that he had been in practice in Poplar, East London for many years. It had been a very busy panel practice with very long hours. Eventually sheer exhaustion and a troublesome wife prompted him to move to this much quieter spot near the sea. It was a relief, he said, to smell ozone instead of fish suppers and crowded humanity. The view of the sea was infinitely preferable to the grimy chimney pots of Poplar too. He solved his domestic problem by paying his wife an adequate annuity to stay away from his new practice. Hmm, thought Sandy, another doctor with a troublesome wife. Well, at least that wouldn't give him a problem this time!

Dr Grant then explained that unexpectedly his practice here had grown and he himself was now needing a break, hence sending for a locum.

In hopes of a semi-retired life, he had put up a very small plate with only his name on it. But this retiring plate, this modest plate, had actually impressed the local residents. They persisted in calling him in professionally much against his will.

Thinking to discourage them he said, he demanded a fee of one guinea, his minimum. To his surprise, they considered that a man of his age and learned appearance, who charged high fees, was worth having as their physician. Willy-nilly he gained a lucrative practice. Sandy, a knowing Scot, guessed that the doctor's thrifty Scottish soul could not then resist the accumulating guineas.

Thus, Dr Grant's practice grew and flourished as he accepted all patients who came to his door. Once again, he found himself overstretched. Rather than give it all up, he decided a locum was the answer so that he could have a rest. And also, give him time to decide what to do. Should he sell, or get an assistant? He definitely needed a vacation to give him time to work it out.

He then suggested that he stay on for a few days to introduce Sandy to those patients who might prove troublesome.

This gave Sandy an opportunity to take proper stock of the doctor. He realized that it was mainly his old fashioned and badly cut suit hanging on his thin stooping frame that had given him the seedy look. But Dr Grant had a sage air and serious grey eyes and inspired confidence in his patients. He had an aura about him which tended to create a feeling of wholesomeness and trust.

He had some very definite ideas on the attitude of the doctor to a patient. He advised, 'Be observant, give the patient the impression that you are wholly interested in him. Be cautious. Never name the disease in case you have to revise the diagnosis. Side-step the question.' Sandy had certainly learned about that one. 'Always remember,' he said, 'sick people are wholly wrapped up in their own particular ailment and think that you can be equally beguiled.'

Dr Grant would sit down at a patient's bedside and patiently listen to a long preamble followed by a discourse on their disease and often a history of the doctor who had failed to cure them. He never made any comment or criticism but went on to condole with them and prescribe the requisite treatment.

At first, Sandy found it irksome to adapt to these methods after the pace and hurry-scurry of panel practice where diagnosis and the prescribing of treatment could only take a few minutes. But now, with only ten visits per day he gradually learned to spend more time on individual cases. Nevertheless, he did find that sitting listening to the patient having his guinea's-worth of his time when he had already decided both diagnosis and treatment in the first five minutes, bored him to distraction.

Sandy had also developed rather an 'ought to' opinion regards people ignoring or dismissing all the benefits offered of immunization, vaccination, free health and medical advice from Radio Doctors and Medical Officers of Health, all of which he discussed with Dr Grant.

But the doctor, although perfectly aware of these benefits held that the individual is the best judge of what treatment he should enjoy. Also, if he wanted just a tonic or some patent medicine or other, let him have it if it made him happy. Dr Grant, was patently a fair-minded man.

Making these mental adjustments was, Sandy thought wryly, all part of the job.

The good doctor though, was highly averse to unqualified and persuasive quacks and was doughty in his criticism of them. He regaled Sandy with several instances of their swindling tricks and one in particular; a dire story that involved a patient of his which, Sandy gathered, had obviously seared his soul. Sandy got the story in full.

He'd had an urgent call one morning; the agitated wife of a patient of his, Mr. Bailey who was in great pain with his leg.

Dr Grant had seen him all too frequently for a condition known as *mus articularis*, a loose body, usually a piece of articular cartridge floating about within the knee joint which sometimes gets into a position where the knee joint becomes locked. This makes the knee painful and stiff until it moves again.

Mr. Bailey had discussed the possibility of an operation with the doctor several times. Because it usually shifted, Dr Grant urged caution, pointing out that operations on the knee were peculiarly liable to infection, endangering the action of the knee and sometimes the life of the patient so felt this option was not to be taken lightly.

Answering this urgent call out to Mr. Bailey he found him greatly alarmed and in agony with his knee swollen to startling proportions. It was highly inflamed, red and hot to the touch and could only be kept slightly bent. He had severe synovitis. What had happened?

The tale came pouring out. One day when his leg locked as he got to work at the bank, on the worldly advice of a knowing cashier, he made an appointment to see 'a famous bone-setter he knew of; a specialist in bones who knew more than doctors did.'

His telephone call to the famous man stating the urgency of the problem secured him an appointment that day. Since it was on a purely cash basis it was recommended Mr. Bailey bring a considerable sum with him. Mr. Bailey arrived at the West End residence of this very busy man and was impressed by the positive sea of letters, M.D. F.R.C.P. and F.R.C.S. among them, adorning the imposing shiny brass plate of Mr. Grummit, Bone Specialist, who had no right to any of them and unaware that bone-setters did not study or qualify in such things as pathology, bacteriology or even physiology.

In the smart Waiting Room, he was pleased to see Tit-Bits and The Sporting Times which put him at his ease. Mr. Bailey was then ushered into the presence of a charming and glamourous receptionist who took him in to Mr. Grummit, a large man reassuringly dressed in the correct garb with silk tie and wing collar.

No sooner had he lain on the couch when Mr. Grummit, seizing the leg by the thigh and the lower leg in his powerful hands, forcibly flexed the leg in a sudden strong movement, 'thereby naturally' said Dr Grant, 'and unknown to Bailey, crushing into fragments the piece of cartilage trapped between the bones.'

Once the initial pain had passed, Bailey was encouraged to get up and try the leg. To his delight he could move the joint freely.

'There you are,' said the great man. 'Why didn't you come to see me before? The fee is 30 guineas. Have you got it with you?'

Poor Bailey, convinced that the man who had performed this miracle in so short a time was a genius, happily parted with his hard-earned money. He was feeling rather sick but the glamourous 'nurse' kindly gave him a brandy. Still feeling a little off-colour, he walked on up the street able to bend his knee and walk normally, albeit with an occasional twinge, mentally blessing his friend the cashier and this clever man.

Forty-eight hours later, his distracted wife phoned Dr Grant.

The violent method adopted by the bone-setter had lighted up some latent infection, 'no doubt inflamed further by the crushed fragments in the joint capsule,' added Dr Grant drily. 'I then said that I was sorry to inform him that he was going to have to spend many expensive weeks in a nursing home before he could walk again. He was not a happy man.'

As far as Mr. Grummit was concerned, concluded Dr Grant sourly, since he did not see Mr. Bailey again, the 'operation' was entirely successful.

* * *

Finding Sandy an interested and attentive listener, Dr Grant stayed on, possibly because he'd found a fellow Scot and a highlander as well. After the daily round and for Sandy, sadly only a meagre evening meal, he unwound enough to relate how his father was a poor Ross-shire crofter and finding his son showed promise had put forth mighty endeavours to get him the education and opportunities denied himself. The upshot was that Hamish Grant qualified in medicine at Edinburgh University with Honours and after a brief period as House Physician and a short assistantship was able to put 'Physician, Surgeon and Accoucheur' on his brass plate in Poplar. There he toiled unremittingly for over 40 years until his semi-retirement in this practice.

Between reminiscences of his medical experiences which Sandy enjoyed and winding up an ancient gramophone and playing lugubrious Scottish songs, which Sandy did not, the evenings passed and the two days stretched into a fortnight.

The old man, alas, was a rather melancholy man and seemed to have lost his sense of humour too. This troubled Sandy not a little, being himself a chap full of the joys of Spring with a very humourous view of life and humanity.

Casting about in his mind for something to cheer him he told him of his times in the West Indies and Paris. This hit the right note and old Hamish brightened up and said he'd like to see something of the world before he died, then added a gloomy afternote of being too old to travel now, it was too late.

Sandy would have none of it.

'No it isn't! I'll give you a hand to compile an itinerary if you like. Perhaps a cruise to the Mediterranean. It's warmer there and you can see Egypt and the Holy Land and Greece where 'burning Sappho loved and sang.'

'Never mind burning Sappho,' he said, 'but I'd like to see Galilee.'

He didn't like to deter the old doctor by telling him that he'd heard that Galilee was a dull and barren waste.

A few days later Dr Grant came in with some pamphlets on trips to the Holy Land and told his housekeeper to start making preparations for his journey. She remarked rather tartly that it was a daft project at his age and he was bound to be robbed or murdered. So, Hamish lingered.

Then he said, 'My health worries me so I'll take a trip up to Edinburgh first to see my nephew who's a surgeon there. All in good time. Nothing serious you know, just a bit of abdominal pain, but still…'

But the expense seemed to worry him considerably. He confided to Sandy that he was haunted by the poverty of his youth and dreaded to face the future unless sure that he would never have to appeal for help from his poor family.

'Poverty is a dreadful thing MacNeil, dreadful. I'll never let that be my fate. I have had a classic instance of a fall to it,' he said heavily.

'I was called out one evening to one of those grimy tenements in Southend to attend a reportedly aged and infirm man said to be in a very bad way. When I saw this unkempt old man, to my astonishment I recognized him! It was one of my old Edinburgh Professors. I was appalled! Such a man in this state of decrepitude, and at this frightful pass! – He'd always been a fine figure of a man and a man of substance!'

Dr Grant then went on to tell Sandy how well he remembered the Prof's palatial Adam house in Moray Place where he used to entertain his senior students. He was renowned for his hospitality. Any final year student in Arts, Medicine or Divinity was assured of a warm welcome, a hot supper, plenty of beer and a sing-song. The last he knew of him was that on his retirement he'd moved to the South of France with plans to travel all over the Mediterranean.

'I just had to ask him how it was he was now in these straits. Gross extravagance, the Professor told me. He said he had no other excuse. He'd inherited his money but was never taught to value it and so he was never capable of regulating his finances. They always seemed inexhaustible to him. 'Didn't know until too late that it had all gone,' he said. 'I'd run through the lot! So here I am Hamish in *this* little hell hole.'

'It was hard to believe! Apparently a highly indulgent life of travel and good living, and especially convivial and very expensive company. Not a thought to the cost or consequences. All he had left,' continued the doctor sadly, 'were a few of his beautiful books, Plato, Aristotle, Lucretius, Aristophanes, – the remnants of a once fine classical library. They were all the company he had now and one frowzy room to live in.' He shook his head. 'I got my Bank to send him a weekly sum but alas, MacNeil, old habits die hard. He squandered it all, mostly on the drink. I eventually discovered that one night a policeman found him lying on a wet pavement, in the rain, cold and obviously very drunk. The police had no idea who the poor drunk was, so he was taken to the local institution where he contracted lobar pneumonia. By the time I found all this out, the poor Professor was dead. The end of a reckless life MacNeil. Ah, reckless indeed,' he sighed.

Dr Grant was adamant that he would never, ever be reduced to this state. It was plain that he was determined to hang on grimly to his money, teetotalism and respectability. Sandy hoped he wouldn't let this frugal view weigh with him and scotch his visit the Holy Land.

ᴅ Chapter 8 ᴄ

Sandy had been in bed for about an hour when the night bell rang. He got up slowly and unwillingly, fumbling for the light switch and his dressing gown and ambled downstairs. But the old doctor was there before him and already talking to the person at the door. He asked the messenger in and signed to Sandy to come into the adjoining room.

'You remember that case we attended today? The fat chap who complained of flatulence and breathlessness? His son tells me his father looks as if he's had a heart attack. He has his motor bike and sidecar with him so I suggest you go right away without waiting to dress. If you wait a minute, I'll get you something to put over your pyjamas while you get your bag.'

Sandy went into the surgery for some coramine and a syringe wondering what the doctor would fetch to cover his night attire. He re-appeared carrying an enormous fur coat and a large matching fur hat.

'See these? I got them off a Russian who couldn't pay his bill, so here, put them on.'

With the doctor's help Sandy got into the coat which came right down to his feet and was so voluminous, he felt quite lost in it. He crammed on the fur hat and they all had a good laugh at his appearance. He somehow got into the side car and clutching his black bag to his chest, they sped off into the damp night.

On arrival the son said for Sandy to go straight in and up to the bedroom, the front door was open. He would put his bike in the shed.

He wandered into the hall stumbling over the folds of the heavy Russian coat. Hearing no sound, he hoisted it as best he could and made his way upstairs where he saw, through an open door, a body stretched out face upwards but half under a bed.

The man had the intense stillness of the dead but in order to examine him properly he tried to drag the body out from under the bed by tucking his hands into the man's armpits. As he did so he unexpectedly saw himself in a pier glass and startled himself considerably and nearly dropped the body. He suddenly realised that he presented a quite ghastly spectacle! With his hair plastered over his face under the enormous hat and great swathes of dark fur in heavy folds all the way down to his feet and clutching a dead body, he looked positively ferocious!

Hearing a sound on the stair he half turned, to confront the pale horrified face of a young woman coming up. Her mouth opened in a scream and she fell headlong down again. Hastily dropping his burden, he bunched up the coat and dashed down to find her already in the arms of her brother, moaning about seeing the Devil taking her father away and then promptly fainting. He tore the hat off his head and hastily pushed the hair off his face in the hope that when she came to, she would no longer identify him as Old Nick.

'I think it was your get-up Doctor that did it,' said the boy. 'Is she hurt?'

'No,' said a relieved Sandy after a brief examination. 'She'll be alright soon,' and held some sal volatile to her nostrils. As the girl came to, she continued to look at Sandy a little wildly so he explained as gently as he could how it came about as a doctor, he was wearing such an extraordinary outfit.

Going up to the bedroom again with the son, it took considerable effort for the two of them to get the body onto the bed. No-one, thought Sandy, who hasn't lifted a dead person has any idea of the weight, the dead weight of a corpse, especially an old, œdematous, flabby one as this poor man was. Between them they did what they could and went downstairs.

Having broken the unhappy news of his death to the rest of the family, he asked the boy to drive him home. He did not resume the hat until he was well away from the house.

Holding the fort one morning, Sandy met a very excited little man at the door demanding to see Dr Grant. His name was Smith he told Sandy, then blurted out, 'My wife is having one of her queer turns! But Dr Grant understands her. I think this is a case for a man older than you Doctor, if I may say so without giving offence.'

'Dr Grant is out at the moment. I'd be quite happy to come to your wife.'

They were standing at the door having this discussion when a prolonged screech of maniacal laughter came from the house opposite. 'Oh, Lord, I think you *had* better come Doctor – while we are waiting for Dr Grant!'

Sandy left a note for Dr Grant asking him to follow him when he came in, and crossed the road in the anxious husband's wake. He unlocked the front door and ushered Sandy into the sitting room before disappearing. To his mild astonishment, he saw a middle-aged woman standing with her back to the window without a stitch of clothing on.

In spite of her bizarre appearance, she seemed perfectly at ease and asked if he would like a whisky and soda, as if she was asking if he'd like a cup of tea in normal circumstances. He deemed it best to humour her, so agreed.

'I knew you would, being a Scotchman. Anything for nothing eh?'

She said this with a charming smile and went to the sideboard to fetch the liquor. It was a unique experience being served with a drink by a woman in the nude and he fervently hoped Dr Grant would arrive very soon and relieve him of the incubus of entertaining this very daft lady.

She handed him the glass and asked if he knew that she was a skilled acrobat. Whereupon she sprang up and seized the candelabrum suspended from the centre of the ceiling and started swinging about on it in imminent danger of bringing the whole thing, including herself, crashing to the ground. Startled into immobility, Sandy felt he was in a surrealist picture, a doctor sitting in a corner holding a glass of whisky and a naked woman performing on a gas bracket.

Thankfully he heard the door bell and to his infinite relief Dr Grant arrived.

'You don't seem to be dealing with this situation very well,' he said drily as Mrs. Smith crashed to the floor bringing the bracket with her and a portion of the ceiling. Sandy was too shaken to make an immediate reply but intended to give him an early opinion of some aspects of general practice!

The maid was then told to bring blankets in which they wrapped the unresisting woman, her sudden and painful descent having somewhat sobered her. They laid her on a settee and then the old doctor showed his skill in dealing with a refractory patient. He spoke to her in a firm but kindly manner telling her she must obey him and put on her clothes.

'The maid will help you dress and then you will do exactly as I say.' His firmness and determined but gentle manner had the desired effect. She meekly allowed the maid to dress her and lead her out to the car which had just arrived to take her to the nursing home for her usual treatment.

'She'll be alright there,' Dr Grant reassured Sandy. 'They are good people, kindly but firm. Thank God, not like the old days of padded cells and the like.'

Some time later, Sandy called to see Mrs. Smith after her discharge from the nursing home. She served him this time with tea and from her perfectly normal demeanour no-one would suspect her of anything but the utmost propriety. Fortunately, to his relief, she had no recollection of her strange behaviour.

* * *

One day the old doctor was enlarging on his *bête noir*, the quack, whom, he was reiterating, he comprehensively loathed, as they were trundling along the London Road in his ancient tourer.

He was driving; his approved speed being 25 miles an hour at the most, he didn't like Sandy's style of driving at all. They stopped outside a patient's house adjoining a large Nursing Home. At that moment a glossy Rolls Royce, complete with liveried chauffeur, slid noiselessly up, the bumpers almost touching the weather-beaten old car.

'Talk of angels!' said Dr Grant.

They watched the chauffeur descend looking pompous and then hold the car door open while a distinguished-looking man alighted. He was tall, with aquiline features and greying temples. He was immaculately dressed in morning coat, striped trousers and top hat.

'Did you see that?' exclaimed Dr Grant. 'Did you *see* it?'

'Golly!' said Sandy. 'The beau ideal of the Harley Street Specialist!'

'Exactly!' said Dr Grant. 'And the biggest quack in the profession! That's Wilshire. He looks grand, doesn't he? The women adore him and he can't even give a dental anæsthetic properly! – but his bedside manner I believe leaves nothing to be desired.'

'You're jealous Doctor,' smiled Sandy.

'Of course I'm jealous, but I wouldn't have his conscience for the world! Remind me to tell you later about 'Abrams Box.'

At about nine o'clock, came Dr Grant's nightly ritual. Going to his sideboard, he unlocked it and took out a

whisky bottle. He then poured himself out about 4 fingers
of the welcome elixir, replaced the bottle and re-locked
the sideboard. Alas, to Sandy's chagrin there was never an
offer of even a dram for him.

Having added about an equal amount of water to his
glass, Dr Grant sat down and sipped the usquebaugh with
relish. He had been careful to explain that he was dead
against alcohol in any form and had been practically a
teetotaler all his life, but he found in later years that this
noggin of whisky helped him sleep. Like all teetotalers, he
regarded it as medicine, but that did not detract from his
evident enjoyment of the forbidden beverage.

'I shall now,' he said, 'give you a little encomium of Dr
Wilshire.'

'Did you say encomium, Doctor?' asked Sandy
facetiously.

'Don't be a fool. I want to point out that Wilshire looks
down on the general practitioner. He goes in for the higher
flights. I have no idea what his activities were before he
came here but evidently, he had heard or read of Abrams'
Box. This box was invented by a Californian physician
named Abrams, who attributed to the box the most
amazing prognostications. It could not only diagnose a
patient's ailment but also suggest the line of treatment.
Wilshire determined to go to the fount of knowledge,
Abrams himself, and secure this wondrous box. Sound's
like a fairy-tale doesn't it? He brought back quite a few of
these boxes from America and made it known by his own
diverse methods that he was the fortunate possessor of
Abrams' famed apparatus. Its fame had already reached
England, – mostly through the press of course,' he added,

his face a picture of derision, 'so Wilshire soon had plenty of patients and had acquired a large impressive house which was perfect as a Nursing Home for his new treatment and his miraculous box. The contraption had a series of little knobs with wires attached and these wires would lead to their mouths, or vaginas, or other orifices or parts affected by the malady, the patient lying there and looking and feeling I imagine, perfectly idiotic. The thing itself looked a bit like an old- fashioned crystal set but little was to be seen bar the wires and the little knobs they were secured to. It seems that faith, – reputed to move mountains, – in the healing powers of the apparently electronic vibrations, was alleged to cure any disease from pernicious anæmia to cancer!'

The doctor took a sustaining sip from his glass but Sandy felt that, going by his fulminating eye, the soothing qualities of the whisky were being a little wasted. He however, was rather enjoying this tale of blatant chicanery though careful to conceal his amusement since Dr Grant was decidedly contemptuous of the whole sham.

'So,' he continued, 'wonder of wonders, by the simple expedient of dropping a spot of the patient's blood onto a piece of blotting paper and placing it in the box, the indicator would show the location of the trouble. To scotch the disease, all that was required was to lead a wire to the affected part from one of the knobs and the electronic vibrations did the rest. It was apparently a rare treat for Dr Wilshire's patients, and strangely, the majority of the sufferers were women, – to have this handsome and distinguished-looking man adjusting wires to their vaginas or other orifices as he murmured words of encouragement while tactfully and deprecatingly accepting their cash offerings of anything from 50 to 100 guineas. But,' and now a small satirical smile lit Dr Grant's features, 'an article in a Medical Journal put the lid on Dr Wilshire and anyone else using Abrams' Box! At the request of several practitioners a committee had been formed to investigate the claims for the contraption. The box itself was found to contain nothing more than would be found in a child's electrical toy and as Abrams himself might have said, 'it was complete bunk!' The blood of a tom cat was placed in the box and the indicator diagnosed 'twin pregnancy.' Now there's a physiological phenomenon! When the press took up the exposure, Dr Wilshire thought it expedient to make a hasty exit before Abrams' box of tricks got too well-known for its true worth.'

'So, how come we saw him today going in to that nursing home?' asked Sandy.

'He came back a few weeks ago after a prudent sojourn in the wilderness, planning, one supposes, his next move. No doubt he's thought of some other 'incredible treatment' to gull the public. He has proved himself a man of infinite resource. He has re-named the place 'Jehovah's Temple' and has been seen down at the local meeting house. What he's up to is anyone's guess but time will tell. So, you see,' continued the worthy doctor, 'if you don't want to spend a lifetime in the laborious application of your medical knowledge you should indulge in some hocus pocus which will intrigue the public and for which you will certainly obtain higher fees and probably more kudos.'

With this final admonition the doctor finished his whisky with an appreciative smack of the lips, and rising to his feet and with a slightly tipsy look, declaimed, 'Now is the time for all good doctors to go to bed.'

The following morning the doctor announced his intention to travel to Edinburgh. He said he'd spent an unhappy night; after the soothing effect of the whisky had worn off the pain in his stomach had returned with increasing intensity. He had now decided to travel north to get his surgeon nephew's opinion on his ailment. Sandy agreed.

As he saw him off on the train it was clear that the doctor's colour, never particularly good, had worsened. Sandy said he hoped the surgeon's report would be a good one and that he'd then be able to continue on to the Holy Land.

It was some three weeks later that the housekeeper announced one afternoon that there was a taxi at the door and that the doctor was back.

He was indeed back but looking very ill as he entered the house. Almost apologetically Sandy said, 'You haven't been abroad then?'

'No. No I have not been after all. I have been no further than Edinburgh.' He sank wearily into an armchair while the housekeeper took care of his luggage.

'I shall never see the world now my boy. It's too late. I've left it too late.'

Sandy's heart sank. 'Why, you are not so old that you can't,' he said, endeavouring to be cheerful, although looking at him, he did fear the worst.

'No,' he continued. 'Like many others less well-informed I have suspected my disease all along but I've been unwilling to accept the inevitable,' he said in a resigned voice. As he raised his head Sandy saw how ashen and gaunt he looked. His expression was quite bleak. This was not good, Sandy thought.

In a tone which combined despair and acquiescence he murmured, 'I am condemned to death MacNeil. Death by Cancer. After my nephew examined me, and he was very thorough, he suggested an X-ray. I knew he wasn't thinking of an ulcer in that moment, my symptoms didn't point to that and when I questioned him more fully, he seemed reluctant to give me a diagnosis.

I said 'I am a doctor, a surgeon like yourself. You think I have a malignant growth in the stomach.' I persisted and told him I wasn't afraid. All I could get him to say was, 'Wait until we see the X-ray film, Uncle, please.'

In the end he had to admit the truth but when it came home to me that I was a victim of the foul disease, I was shocked beyond measure. How often have I diagnosed that malady in a patient and had to tell the relatives of my conclusions. I always felt a certain amount of sympathy but not stirred to my vitals as I was when I realized I was condemned. I knew everything it entailed, the pain, the distress, the interminable suffering and the inevitable end.'

Sandy tried to tell him that maybe he was too pessimistic. 'X-ray alone isn't sufficient for a diagnosis, perhaps a laparotomy?'

'My boy, you are trying to be kind. You are bound to have noticed my colour and I have not always been this thin so I was wasting before you came. I do not deceive myself. I know my end is come. It does not matter now, I mean about my travels abroad,' he continued drearily. 'Just like any amateur I've left this thing too late for operative treatment. Until now, I found it difficult to comprehend the attitude of the patients who have a suspicion they have cancer. They keep on hoping for the best and postpone a visit to the doctor until it's too late for surgical help.' He fell silent for a while as if considering what further to say.

Sandy said nothing. He was profoundly sorry.

'My nephew expects me to place myself in his care as soon as I find a purchaser for my practice. By the way,' he said, looking up at Sandy with something like the former keenness in his grey eyes.

'What about you buying it?'

'That depends on how much you want for it,' he replied, startled into an answer.

Dr Grant took out a notebook and pencil and scribbled for a while.

'At a rough estimate, the income approaches £3,000 a year, the house is worth say, £950. As there is no panel, I could let you have the practice for one and a half year's purchase instead of the usual 2 years so that would mean I'd need £5,800 cash.'

Great Heavens! thought Sandy, looking in astonishment at this old man with but a few months to live but still in the throes of his ruling passion, cash!

'Listen Dr Grant. My total assets are in the region of 30 quid. If I had that kind of money I wouldn't buy a practice, I'd retire to the South Sea Islands and do no more work for the rest of my life!'

I should have known, he thought, a tad riled. 'Well, now I must be off, I have my visits to make,' and made good his escape leaving the old man still scribbling away in his notebook.

The doctor had no difficulty in finding a purchaser. In a few weeks a smart blue saloon car arrived with the new owner of the practice, a very la-di-da and opulent young man, a striking contrast to the vendor but no doubt having other equally attractive qualifications. But to Sandy's casual observation they seemed more of a financial nature than otherwise.

The old doctor had had to leave for Edinburgh long before the transaction was complete. Perhaps, Sandy thought wryly, the worry of those pounds sterling hadn't helped his complaint.

The Agent took over and paid him his fee as *locum tenens* on the day that La-di-da gave him his congé. He looked at his tiny cheque and wished that some thoughtful Member of Parliament would evolve some scheme to make it easier for enthusiastic new doctors with limited funds to acquire practices, instead of La-di-da's with money to burn getting all the pickings without any effort. In lieu of wasting his time in wishful thinking, he made all haste for the Strand and his Medical Agent.

Some time later, he saw Hamish Grant's Will published in a daily paper. He had left £29,560. Poor Hamish had certainly left a fortune but as far as Sandy knew, had not visited the Holy Land.

◗ Chapter 9 ◖

Sandy was unable to show the Medical Agency that he possessed any capital nor did he evince any desire to raise capital in the usual way to buy a practice, so he was placed on the list of permanent locums. For the most part, this did keep him regularly in work.

Through his visits to the Agency, he often met a familiar face, other medicos in the same boat, no money and poor prospects of a practice. A young doc from Sheffield whom he sometimes had a beer or two with, nearly got caught out by a certain type of financial agent who circularised newly-fledged doctors. His northern caution prompted him into making close enquiries of other locums into what these letters offered. What he learned made him sheer off in time. He told Sandy that it was nothing short of a conspiracy, a conspiracy to mortgage the life and soul of any poor young doctor likely to be vicitimised.

These agents, in their letters, offer to any doctor who hasn't got the necessary capital, a project by which he can obtain a practice of his own. The Agent is a kind and obliging man; you select the practice and if it is a reliable one, he will buy it for you with his own good money. As he is not exactly a philanthropist, he must ensure that he will be repaid.

To make certain of this, the intending purchaser is recommended to insure his life for a substantial sum in the Agent's favour, the doctor being liable for the premium. If he possesses any capital at all, he must hand that over to help things along. The quarterly cheque received from the National Insurance Committee must also be handed over to the agent in legal form as soon as the doctor gets it. This helps to pay off the capital sum advanced. The agent may even need a portion of the fees paid by non-panel or private patients.

All the rest is the doctor's very own. The 'rest' consisting of what small proportion of the private takings is left. Out of this of course, he has to pay the insurance premium, the interest on the sum advanced by the kindly Agent, general expenses, stuff for his dispensary, personal expenditure, food, transport of some sort etc. But the financier is not too hard. Although the rate of interest is 15%, he doesn't ask the hard-working doctor to keep paying for the term of his natural life, only for a period of say fifteen to twenty years. If the doctor survives long enough without blowing his brains out or dying of drink, why the practice is his! It's too bad if he doesn't survive as the agent has the whole trouble of selling the practice again to the next sucker.

No. Sandy had no desire to raise capital in this way.

Of course he could always get a job as an assistant. This is a doctor who hires himself out for a salary to an established practitioner. From all reports he discovered that the assistant is the 'dog's-body,' the perfect term, Sandy thought. He's reckoned a learner so why should he complain if the boss uses him to do all the dirty work;

night calls, confinements, miscarriages, the calls coming in at meal times, accidents, suicides, long distance visits....' Furthermore, in case the said assistant is tempted to try any funny stuff like branching out in the same district on his own account, he has to sign a Bond. The Bond threatens him with the severest penalties if he makes any move to start a practice on his own within a radius of x miles and within a period of stated years, in his employer's neighbourhood.

With the reliance on the private patient and the consequent commercialisation of the professional, the internecine warfare between doctors was a serious problem especially in the smaller towns.

So, the assistant's prospects are nil and he seldom if ever gets any increase in his salary and he has little or no standing with the boss's wife or the patients.

No. Sandy didn't fancy being an assistant.

But what about being an assistant with view? This means a doctor who gets a tiny share and pays for it out of his salary. The 'view' is a view to partnership so the amount of cash he can stump up, will determine how distant the view is.

No. Sandy didn't fancy that either.

And where did Sandy gather all this information? He got it from the acquaintances he made in the waiting room of the Medical Agency and they were mostly locums both young and old. After the secretary had distributed any jobs going, the remainder of them would gravitate to the bodega nearby.

With foaming tankards charged with good ale, they discussed their vicissitudes, the fluctuations and fleetingness of any kind of love life, criticized their employers and swapped any useful information going. They even tossed the idea about in favour of their Trades Union the BMA, finding those with no capital, a free practice or two. Or why didn't the Government make them a branch of the Civil Service and pay them a salary, keeping them in steady employment and so make good use of their talents? They all talked a lot but of course got nowhere.

Another fruitful topic for close examination and complaint was the Lodging House Landlady, the main feature of life between locums. Someone who, at the low prices they could afford between jobs, could make both food and lodging incredibly uninteresting and with everything edible shoved into the frying pan no matter what, she concentrated all the hatred of her own poverty in increasing the discomfort of her guests.

And, they cried, 'the destruction of the alimentary tract!' The prevailing digestive conditions among the lodgers, they found, were gastric and duodenal ulcers, gall-stones, pernicious anæmia and bowel cancer.

These meetings became a regular habit. In fact, they called it The Locum Tenens Club, no admission fee. Sometimes they forgathered there in the evenings at a table that Jessie, one of the barmaids, kept for them when she found out they were members of the Medical Profession. She had a soft spot for doctors had Jessie. She had once been close to one of the housemen when she'd been a probationer nurse in one of the London Hospitals. She had made the mistake of being caught *in flagrante delicto* with the houseman, with the result that she was now dispensing beer instead of 'the mixture three times a day.'

Sandy, ever drawn to people of singular character, point of view or shaped interestingly by their experiences or culture, found just such a choice spirit there in Hymie Finkel.

He was a little man, a Jew but insisted he was a Yidd and naturally called himself so. His home was in the Whitechapel district, where he and his brother Sol, were, as he described it, 'dragged up.' Old Finkel, the father, originated in Russia. Coming to this country, he had started his career as a hawker of doubtful fruit with his two little boys as equally doubtful assistants, who when not devouring the contents of the barrow, were engaged in bawling out their parent's wares. In time, old Finkel abandoned fruit hawking for the cigar business, which prospered so well he was able to send his boys into the professions; Sol into the Law and Hymie into medicine. Hymie was a good student but only went so far as a Licenciate of the Society of Apothecaries.

Sandy asked him why he hadn't gone on to take his MB and a surgical degree.

'Oh, it's just a waste of time and money!' he replied. 'What do the public know of Degrees? All I needed to get on in the profession was to be able to call myself Doctor, and as an L.S.A. I can do that. You know as well as I do that it's only a courtesy title. The only man as you know entitled to call himself Doctor is an M.D. a Doctor of Medicine. I once heard two blokes arguing about their respective doctors. One boasted that his was an M.D. and the other said, 'That ain't nothin' chum. My doctor has more letters after his name than that! He's an [4]L.R.C.P., M.R.C.S., M.C.O.G.!' He obviously didn't know that L.R.C.P. and M.R.C.S. are known as the English conjoint and I suppose that's the simplest degree you can get, whereas the M.C.O.G isn't a degree at all, but a diploma or something presented if you do so many baby cases in Dublin.'

'Are you sure of that Hymie?' asked Sandy.

'Pos-it-ive-ly!' he said and ordered two more ports.

One evening, Sandy and a bunch of them having missed the boat at the Medical Agency that day, got settled with suitable potations to dispel the slight gloom. One of them, Harrison, was a large young man with a dark and glossy beard he was rather proud of, which he said, made him look suitably portentous should the occasion call for it; it made no end of a good impression on the patient. But, he said, not on the last doctor whose practice he'd taken charge of.

'In fact, no sooner arrived and greeted than the old badger was damned derogatory, saying beards were grossly unhygienic. Well, that put my back up to start with,' he said. 'Then he went into a lecture on the shocking propensity that locums had for alcohol, just like a schoolmaster admonishing a bratty schoolboy, and his 'extreme displeasure and determination that it was not going to happen while he and his wife were away on their holiday' and he'd locked up what little he allowed in the house in the sideboard and was taking the key. Well,' continued Harrison, 'one night me and a pal met for a beer or two to pep ourselves up after a particularly hard day. I told him the sad tale and then I had a brainwave. 'We could take the back off the sideboard and get a snifter and put it back later!' 'Good idea! said Bill. 'Lead on McDuff!' Well, we got the back off with a screwdriver alright, and you wouldn't believe it! It was chock full of hooch! 'The old hypocrite!' cries Bill. Well, chaps, suffice it to say, that we two had the jolliest evenings that practice ever had! We did it full justice!'

Amid the roars of laughter Harrison cried, 'Our only regret is that we never saw the old skinflint's face when he got back and unlocked it!'

◗ Chapter 10 ◖

The following day two of their number being first in line, had got lucky. A bunch of them with Sandy and Hymie, went straight round for consolation to The Locum Tenens Club. They found their usual table and set up a round of ports and beers.

Jessie paused at their table and said, 'Hymie, wots become of Dr McInnes, ain't seen 'im for donkey's years.'

'Funny your asking that. I was talking about Willie only the other day. He went to the Gold Coast, West Africa y'know.'

'Coo-er! The White Man's Grave innit? Wot a place to send poor Willie,' she tutted. ''e was a nice kid, Willie. Only one glass o'port and 'e was as tight as a tick!' Jessie laughed and went off to her beer-serving duties.

Looking round the table, Hymie said. 'If you've time to listen practitioners, I think I'd like to tell you the story of Willie McInnes, because it points a moral and adorns a tale.'

They all agreed, suitably intrigued. Hymie was a born raconteur and always entertaining. Besides, they were happy at the distraction and they could see Hymie was raring to go.

'It's quite a longish story so I do warn you.' he added. They all nodded their interest and ordered another round to launch the tale.

'You need to understand,' said Hymie, 'this tale is mostly second-hand as it concerns my brother Sol, the lawyer. He was able to piece the drama together, see? Sol, as you know has his legal offices in the Whitechapel Road, but he lives up the Thames at Waldegrave. Now I don't know if you've ever visited Waldegrave-on-Thames but in the winter months, the river rises and slops over half the town and also treats the town to cold, thick and penetrating fogs. No doubt you've been up the Thames in the summertime when everything in the garden is lovely, but if you really want to undermine your health, try spending a winter there! One particular November,' continued Hymie, 'I think it was 1925, Waldegrave had a spell of that cold foggy weather, so Sol, being on the fat side and bronchial, took hardly with it and developed a cough. On a Saturday afternoon, being his half day he was at home in his little study writing up some papers, when Ruthie, that's his wife you know, got a bit windy hearing him cough, cough, cough. 'Solly,' she says, 'I'm going to send for the doctor to examine your chest, that's an awful cough!' 'Don't be silly!' says Sol, 'I always get a cough in November,' and went on with his writing. 'Anyway,' says Ruthie, 'I'm going to take your temperature.' Off she toddled to the bathroom and fetched a thermometer from the medicine chest and stuck it in Sol's mouth. Sol was more interested in his writing though. 'It's not a cigarette Solly! Keep it in your mouth!' cries Ruthie. When she removed it, she gave a shriek of dismay. 'Solly! You're ill, it's 101! Come on get to bed!' 'Wha-at!' cries Sol. '101? Get the doctor Ruthie!' and immediately tottered off to bed while Ruthie bustled off to phone the doc. When

Ruthie came back and said there were no doctors available, to say Sol was furious was to put it mild! They'd all gone off to the International at Twickenham, according to the dispenser and didn't know when they'd be back!' Hymie joined in the general laughter.

'Sol sits up in bed and bellows, 'Damn Dr Smallweed! *And* his partners, Greenbank and Whyte! What they need in this town is another doctor in opposition to stir them up!' Ruthie calmed him down a bit and said the dispenser could get their young assistant to come, if he would do, a chap called McInnes, a Scotsman. 'He'll do,' said Sol. 'They say Scotchmen make good doctors.' The upshot was that Willie pulled him through lobar pneumonia and Sol got very attached to Willie as a result. He then decided to do the boy some good, – and himself at the same time if possible. When he found that Willie's prospects with Smallweed and Co were exactly nil, Sol made a proposition, in effect, that Willy, not having signed a Bond for some strange reason, should resign from Smallweed's and start in opposition to the firm. He could have Sol's study as a consulting room and his dining room as a waiting room, and furthermore, a nice brass plate with Dr W. McInnes and other suitable inscriptions would be set on the gatepost flanking Sol's own brass plate, Soloman Finkel, Solicitor. You see he wasn't above doing a little extra legal work at his home address. After a lot of argument but with considerable trepidation Willie agreed but he insisted on being strictly ethical by handing a letter of resignation to the senior partner plus stating his intention of setting up a practice in Walgrave -on-Thames. The trio treated this letter as rather a joke and told

McInnes to get on with it, the idea of small fry like Willie McInnes starting up in opposition to the powerful firm of Smallweed and Co was hardly taken seriously. In fact, they gave him a week's salary in lieu of notice – but they reckoned without Soloman Finkel Solicitor....'

'I say Hymie,' Sandy interjected 'That was pretty decent of him. Your brother sounds a really good honest chap.'

'No, he certainly is not!' countered Hymie laughing. 'He's the biggest swindler I know but he knows how many beans make five and he can sail closer to the law without foundering than any legal merchant East of Aldgate, that I know! I agree that Sol wanted to repay Smallweed for allowing a Yiddish gentleman like Sol to die of pneumonia while he went to rugby matches but he needed Willie badly. Some of Sol's schemes see, required a good doctor to give the necessary backing in court in certain kinds of compensation cases that Sol specializes in. You know the kind of case. The Company doctor says the man's malingering but Sol needs a doctor to prove that the plaintiff's back will never, never recover from that fall down the hatchway. Sol can bellow in his best huckster's voice that it is a gross libel to say that the man was drunk, but it's the doctor's word which decides whether the thousand quid asked for is awarded. Sol can then be sure of a substantial rake-off. That's the kind of doctor Sol envisaged in simple Willie, see?'

'Great Scot Hymie! Had he no gratitude for Dr McInnes pulling him through pneumonia?' Sandy asked.

'But certainly,' said Hymie. 'Sol set out to make Willie a practitioner in the shortest possible time and this he did by becoming a perambulating tout. Wherever he went, to the Barber's, the local, the Post Office, in fact anywhere the chance presented itself, Sol boosted Dr McInnes. He told all and sundry of the wonderful doctor he had allowed to start at his house, and conversely slated Smallweed and Co as a bunch of quacks. Willie had no idea of all this touting mind. He would have been dead against it. He was just surprised and happy at the large number of eager patients coming to him. Never questioned it.'

'Ye gods!' said Harrison, with a laugh. 'Smallweed and henchmen must have been hopping mad!'

'They were!' said Hymie grinning. 'When their quarterly cheque and accounts came in a few months later things started to hum! There was a big chunk missing from their panel and they guessed who'd done the carving! Their dispenser, who'd been acting as self-appointed spy had been warning them with daily reports, but Smallweed had ignored him. Now, drastic measures were called for against this upstart McInnes. Alas, despite appeals to the Medical Protection Society, the BMA and even the Ethical Secretary of the BMA, nothing could be done. 'Can't do a thing; no contract; no Bond.' Smallweed was fairly smouldering by this time. He'd been convinced that the whole power of the profession would have lined themselves up on his side. Then he thought, 'Ah! the Medical Officer of Health! The notorious sticker-of-his-nose-into-other-people's-business, Allways-East!

'Dr Allways-East is the man for the job!' he told the partners. But when the M.O.H called to reason with this recalcitrant squatter who should he meet, but Sol! Willie was out. The M.O.H. made his first bloomer,' grinned

Hymie. 'He asked Sol if he was the butler. No! he bawled, he was not the butler. When he realized the M.O.H's mission he really exploded. He was the doctor's lawyer and threatened to sue him, Smallweed and Co, the BMA and even the British Medical Council if he didn't hook it and leave Dr McInnes to the quiet and legal pursuit of his practice! Dr. Allways-East was back in his car in no short order and motoring off at speed,' chortled Hymie.

'What came of it then?' asked one of the others. 'Did McInnes get away with it?'

'No, he fell into a trap. He knew nothing of all this y'see. Sol suspected that it was in the wind but Willie was so flattered to receive an invitation to a meeting of the local branch of the BMA of which he was a member that he went to it. And didn't they sock him! Smallweed was chairman and made such a moving speech to the practitioners round the table with Willie at the end, about the iniquity of squatters stealing the bread from the mouths of established doctors and how such conduct pierced at the roots of medical tradition, that they were all glaring at Willie as if he were a pariah. Then they all added their mite and certainly not in Willie's favour. Well,' Hymie went on, 'there was Willie, ruddy-complexioned Scotch boy, bright blue eyes and curly ginger hair who looks the personification of innocence and simplicity but something rose in him that this was going a bit too far! He was ardently wishing Sol was there, so he was a bit nervous but determined to plead his case. 'In my circumstances, with no money, no backers, I have to make a living somehow and I don't see how I can do that except by squatting as you call it. I'm sorry, but I intend to remain in the practice as I am breaking no law.' At that Smallweed jumped up spitting tacks and lost all dignity. 'So, you've broken no law, well we'll break *you*, you little whipper-snapper. We'll circularise all the doctors in this area to the effect that you've been guilty of conduct unbecoming a member of the Medical Profession. You'll never be able to get an anæsthetist if you need one nor any medical help, nor attend any case you send to the Walgrave Cottage Hospital of which *I'm* chairman!' This really put the wind up, poor Willie, but when he described the whole affair to Sol, Sol laughed. 'It's a great big bluff, they can't do a thing to you and if they do, I'll tear them limb from limb! The BMA wouldn't back up such palpable blackmail.' But,' sighed Hymie, 'the rot had set in.'

'Surely they didn't get away with it?' someone cried.

'Well to Willie, 'conduct unbecoming' put him on par with abortionists and blokes erased from the register, so got the wind up proper. Then the M.O.H carted him off to meet his family and tea at his house and did a proper softening-up job on him and convinced him that this really was not on, squatters were beyond the pale and virtually belonged to the criminal classes.'

This was greeted with a chorus of animadversions and complaints on the impossibilities of the whole rotten business and scorn for this below-the-belt treatment of Willie McInnes. They supposed it had it all been too much for him in the end.

'Exactly,' said Hymie. 'He threw the whole thing up, to Sol's great disgust and went into the West African Medical Service.'

'Where I suppose he is now, making lashings of dough,' said Sandy.

'He did make plenty of dough his first trip or tour as they call it.' answered Hymie, 'but if you want to hear the rest of it, we'll need another round, as long as you've got the time to hear it.'

Realizing there was even more to this story, the rest of them agreed to hear it and sent for more ports and beers to oil the thing along and sustain them in readiness. Jessie brought the drinks. 'You blokes are having a proper session tonight! What are you celebrating? But why all the serious faces?'

'Sit down, Jess,' invited Hymie. 'This is the life story of our mutual friend Willie McInnes, so if you want to hear how he's getting on in West Africa, park yourself and listen.'

'Can't sit down that long!' she cried horrified. 'The boss'll mark me! I'll 'ave to 'ear the story some other time.'

◗ Chapter 11 ◖

'For his first stint,' continued Hymie, 'Willie was sent to a place called Tumaki, a place with about 200 whites and thousands of natives, well-paid natives employed in the near-by gold mines. He was allowed a private practice there and soon Willie was doing very well as Government doctor. Every week, he would dump on the counter of the local bank, wads of grubby West African Bank notes and piles of the brassy West African coinage and every month a draft of good proportions was sent to his mother in Scotland. The Africans liked this fresh-complexion, red-headed Scotch lad and brought all their ailments, syphilis, leprosy and a whole bunch of strange tropical diseases to Willie's well-equipped hospital. When he found their money was good and the fees higher and more cheerfully paid than in this country, he even essayed a little surgery like the removal of tumors, circumcision and the like and for this good work quite substantial fees were paid in cash. Willie was happy and glad he had joined the Colonial Medical Service. He reckoned that in a few years he would be able to pack up and buy a decent practice at home – no more squatting. His old mother in the little village of Corrydale in Scotland was equally delighted and took great pride in taking Willie's large monthly draft to the Bank. 'My, my,' said the manager. 'He must be a clever lad, that son of yours to be making all this money at his age!' Naturally it wasn't long before the whole village got to know and while some said behind Mrs. McInnes' back that it was a shame making all that money off the poor blacks, they told her it was splendid.'

'Come off it, Hymie!' Sandy interjected. 'How do you know all this?'

'Knew you'd ask this!' he replied, well-primed by the port. 'Read it in his letters of course,' he answered. 'He wrote regularly to Sol and I heard some of his Africa stunt from Willie himself, but if you really want to know, not so long ago I paid a visit to Corrydale where I culled a few more facts. Incidentally, you'd better order a few more drinks as I intend to break your hearts before this tale is told and weep a few tears of my own, see?'

'Hymie, you're getting bottled so hurry up and tell us the worst before they call time gentlemen please and we get our marching orders,' he said laughing.

Harrison collared some more drinks.

'To continue,' said Hymie. 'After his 12-month tour was up Willie was entitled to four months leave. He came back to London and Sol and I met him for lunch at the Savoy looking good, and fit and well after his sea voyage. We took him to a West End tailor to order some new suits and a nice grey herring-bone tweed overcoat, – happy as a kid he was, to have some money to spend. We planned to have about two weeks jollification till his suits were ready and then he'd be off to Corrydale to see his Ma where he was bound to cut a dash with his West End suits and then tot up his savings, which by all accounts were pretty good by now. But Willie had reckoned without the West African Audit department,' said Hymie lugubriously.

'Sounds ominous Hymie! What's their racket?' asked one of the docs.

'Ah!' said Hymie. 'A very efficient organization that keeps an eagle eye on the finances of all its employees. I heard of it after Willie fell foul of it. The Deputy Director of Medical Services, who lives in the capital, Cracra was informed by a friend of his of the large dollops of cash, as well as his salary that Dr McInnes was sending home to his Ma. The D.D.M.S, obviously a man with a suspicious mind must have thought Willie was up to no good because he decided a transfer to a less lucrative district was in order and marked Willie down for Buncwa, a filthy swamp right out in the bush.'

'Hey, Hymie! That's low! You aren't making this up, are you?' Harrison asked, eyeing him askance.

'Not at all! Willie found out all about it when he got back and was told the news. All behind his back and the deed done. He told Sol in one of his letters of course. Willie was not happy, he'd heard of Buncwa, well-known as a benighted plague spot and so far out it took a train trip and a long flaming-awful trek through the bush in a hammock carried by natives to get there! Well, if I tell you that the living accommodation was a basic dump of hardened mud with no ameneties at all, a mud-walled hospital and ditto nearby compound for the natives, you'll get the picture that greeted Willie. Thanks to the large swamp nearby, he was bitten by tsetse flies before he even got through the door and prayed they didn't give him an immediate dose of sleeping sickness. The only other white man, a palm oil trader, Smithers, lived over three miles away and spent his days in the bush so he was rarely about. The natives were a poor lot, cheap labour hired by the native owners of the cocoa plantations. Sadly, they were very rarely paid. That meant Willie was rarely paid. Of course, the diseases were the same as Tumaki, some even worse and malaria an added hazard. He tried some measure of mosquito control but it was hopeless and the rainy season was extra depressing, water everywhere and electric storms. The tropical heat was suffocating and he constantly dripped sweat. The racket at night from the insects and wildlife nearly drove him frantic. He had no insect screens either. The loneliness was the worst. He had no appetite for the native food or their cooking either and soon found a few whiskies helped with the awful isolation. Alas he had an all too ready source of booze in the native stores which held plenty of liquor, – much loved by the local plantation owners! So, he was fast getting used to it. This was not good for him – but I'm sure you're getting the picture. If you could read some of his letters to Sol who was the only person he could talk to, they'd make your heart bleed as well as make your hair curl, but we are running out of time so I'll move on.

'This is a frightful tale Hymie,' cried Sandy to whom company was essential.

'Hold on,' Hymie replied. 'Eventually he did get quite pally with old man Smithers through their mutual uptake of alcohol. Anyway, the old chap liked him, took pity on him and arranged to exchange more frequent visits which, of course got very boozy. Anyway, one night they got together, but the old man having passed out Willie set off to walk the three miles through the bush back to Buncwa. He started to feel ill and was shuddering badly by the time he staggered home. By the morning, he was so ill that it frightened the houseboy so much that he ran to get Smithers. It was some time though before a rather hungover Smithers got there. It was oppressively hot and he found Willie shuddering and feverish. He'd obviously not been taking his quinine. Willie admitted it and said he'd taken 15 grains of the stuff and another whisky when he got home to mitigate the shivering. Worst thing for him! He was in terrible pain and vomiting, and Smithers saw the urine in his chamber pot was the colour of port wine, – every sign of blackwater fever. He was horrified. Willie had an appalling thirst and though he encouraged him to drink Smithers saw his urine was getting darker and darker. Fatigue, malaria and 15 grains of quinine, – guaranteed to break down his blood! Willie was dazed with pain but of course recognised the dreaded disease and managed to tell Smithers that the only treatment was intravenous bicarbonate of soda. But Willie had no means to do that. This sent the old man off hot-foot to the post office to call Cracra. They said they'd send a doctor with the necessary stuff so he went back to Willie to do what he could to try to get some fluids into him. Poor Willie was rapidly deteriorating, his fever was worse and now there was black blood in his urine. Smithers tried soda bic in water and even goats' milk and fruit juice. By night time and still no sign of the doctor, Willie obviously knew how bad things were and made him promise to write to his mother. By the time the doctor *did* eventually arrive, late the following day, it was too late. Willie had gone into a coma and was now dead. Died not much before the doc arrived in fact.' Hymie shrugged and looked into the dregs of his port. No-one spoke.

Then Sandy said. 'If it isn't a rude question Hymie, how come you know all the ghastly details?'

'Well, from old Smithers. He found Willie's letters from Sol and got in touch with him. The old man was really cut up by Willie's death so wanted to let him know how it had been. He wasn't going to let that go unrecorded, he said. He couldn't very well write that grim stuff to his mother although he did write a letter to her.'

'TIME GENTLEMEN PLEASE!' bawled the potman, banging a thick glass on the counter to emphasize his words. 'Hif you've got 'omes to go to, go to 'em now. TIME GENTS PU-LEASE!'

This brought everyone back with a jolt. They'd all been quite carried away with this unhappy tale. Then Hymie jumped up.

'Oi!' shouted Hymie. 'You think you can bawl? Well, listen to this,' and swaying slightly and taking a deep breath, roared out in his best huckster's voice, 'TER-MARTERS, R-R-R-IPE TER-MARTERS, SIXPENCE A PAHND!'

This uproar broke the slight gloom that had descended on the table. The potman informed Hymie that if he wanted to do any yelling, to do it outside. Jessie urged them to go quietly. She was visibly upset; she'd overheard the last part of Hymie's story.

Once outside all but Sandy and Hymie parted company. The two locums then swayed to a shop doorway at the corner of the Strand. Hymie wanted to get the rest of the tale off his chest.

'After Smithers wrote Sol, I went up to Corrydale,' he said. 'Sol was upset but was too busy with a case, wouldn't want to miss his usual rake off! Well, out of curiosity I had a bit of a snoop round see and it was easy to hear all the gossip. Ma of course had been getting anxious as there were no weekly letters from Willie and no drafts either. Getting in a bit of a state she was, they said. When weeks later she went to the post office again in hope of some post, all she found from Africa was the letter from Smithers and the terrible news. Then a letter from the Colonial Office came and that did it for her, see,' said Hymie. 'I went to see her. Got some of her side of the tale from her too. She was pleased enough to tell me all about her dear Willie and glad he'd had Sol to write to. I tell you Sandy. It cut me up I can tell you. Sol heard later from her neighbour, Mrs. McNab that after such a shock she seemed to lose interest. She said she was past caring and Ma McNab wasn't surprised that she fell ill soon after. She sent for the doc but Ma had contracted pneumonia and had no resistance to fight it. Dead by the end of the week.'

Just as Sandy was wondering what on earth to say, a hawker of fruit moved his barrow to the curb.

'Cor! Stone me, if it isn't Mose!' ejaculated Hymie, rapidly going into the vernacular. 'Wotcher! Look 'ere I'll sell yer fruit for you Mose!' and with that bawled, 'R-R-R-RIPE VICTORIA PLUMS, TUPPENCE A PAHND. VICTORIAAS!'

Hymie's bellow caused a policeman to halt in his stride.

'Nasty little bastid of a 'awker, aint yer? Pipe dahn, will yer? Pipe dahn!' and giving Dr Finkel a baleful look, continued his beat along the Strand.

Sandy decided he'd leave these two hawker pals to their reminiscences and hoped no-one from the ancient body of Apothecaries was around to hear Hymie bawling out fruit at so much A PAHND.

◗ Chapter 12 ◖

After a considerable number of locums in London and various places countrywide, Sandy got a posting and found himself in Yorkshire. It was in the hunting country and he was pleased at this as he was keen to see a real fox hunt having read Surtees, and been greatly entertained by Jorrocks.

By this time, he'd acquired a second-hand Austin Six, keen for the independence of his own transport. It also made it possible for him to readily accept such rural north country locums as this.

The doctor, Dr Flanagan he discovered, had broken both bones in his right forearm down at the wrist, a Colles's fracture. It transpired that this had occurred on the hunting field and Sandy had a sudden irreverent vision of the doc in a ditch with the horse making for home.

On greeting, he informed Sandy that he needed him for two weeks only. A fracture in plaster was neither to keep him from his practice for long nor his hunting, which he called huntin'. This was his abiding passion.

In appearance Flanagan was not at all like Jorrocks. He was what that burly hunting man would have termed 'a cut me down gent.' He was a long thin-gutted man of some 30 odd years, over six foot tall with long flat feet that went flip flop, flippity-flop as he walked and despite his presumably outdoor life his face was thin and pale and his narrow nose seemed to drip permanently.

His whole appearance on first meeting him, was untidy. He was wearing a threadbare dressing gown and looked a miserable object flippity-flopping about in his carpet slippers.

The house was a two-storied unpretentious place. It was very untidy and full of dogs; a dozen or so of spaniels, assorted terriers, mongrels and a dachshund. Sandy was horrified; the furniture showed clear evidence of their activities in the torn tapestry of the settee and armchairs and the sinister stains on the carpet. And the house smelled strongly of animals.

He discovered straight away that these were Mrs Flanagan's passion and she called them doggies. He had a short interview with her, a diminutive lady regarding his accommodation and food when a bull terrier of ferocious aspect lifted his leg unchallenged against the dining room table.

Appalled, Sandy's face immediately registered his disgust and she said hastily that she didn't like her doggies to be upset; she wrote articles on them and even derived an income from describing the habits and maladies of these animals so was very proud and fond of them. She preferred dogs to babies, she said. Neither she nor her husband believed in bringing children into the world who might serve only as cannon fodder. Looking at the doctor, the dogs and the state of the house, Sandy thought it was just as well.

And huntin' he soon realised, interested the doctor far more than did general practice or the practice of medicine.

Looking at Dr Flanagan's visiting list later, Sandy saw that for some inexplicable reason, the majority of his patients were suffering from myocarditis – heart disease. When he remarked on this fact to the doctor, he only got an evasive answer; something about the prevailing rheumatism in these parts. Sandy had yet to discover why it was his private patients only who had heart disease.

In the course of his rounds, he speedily discovered that the myocardial cases simply did not exist. Flanagan, whom Sandy privately now called Flannelfeet, kept them in bed with their bogus ailments while he hunted. They afforded him an income without much trouble.

Sandy was not impressed and felt honour-bound to remonstrate with him. Flanegan didn't agree with him. In any case he said, huntin' was an expensive recreation and he wasn't really interested in these people. What he was aiming at, was to make contact with The County, with people of substance and standing. In short, the Best People. When he had made the proper connections, he would give up his panel and the middle classes. Meanwhile most of his income he said, went into huntin' so it was only a means to an end.

Mrs. Flanagan, whom the doctor habitually bullied and overbore, corroborated this. It cost money to be a member of the Whorfdale Hunt and there were the incidental outlays, horse, groom, stabling and so on, but she was sure that with Barry's personality they would soon be recognized by The County. Sandy now realized that this accounted for the cheap ghastly diet of mainly sausages, chips and tea or watery egg. A far cry, he thought from Jorrock's hot brandy and water followed by barons of roast beef! He couldn't see how such skilly sustained old Flannelfeet for all that huntin'.

He saw that he had a Lady Kirby-Whorf on his list so a visit to her offered some interest. He found that she lived in a lovely old mansion nearby, surrounded by beautiful parkland. As he drove up through the fine park to the mansion, Sandy guessed that she was obviously the most influential of Dr Flanagan's patients, being the local landowner. No doubt the gracious old house ahead was the ancient seat of the Kirby-Whorfs, he thought.

He was shown through a wide stone-pillared hall and up to an immense bedroom where the invalid was propped up with pillows in a four-poster bed. The head of the bed was festooned with innumerable electric flexes with push buttons, presumably to each member of the household staff.

She looked a woman of character and determination, fiftyish, he thought, with thick dark hair and a good complexion. She instantly expressed her disgust at being confined to her bed when she felt quite well and hoped he would let her get up for the approaching Meet of the Whorfdale Hunt. He then heard that until Dr Flanagan found that she suffered from myocarditis, she used to be an active rider to hounds, since when she had been confined to bed with a nurse in attendance.

He had a look at the chart which conveyed nothing out of the ordinary. Although her pulse was slow, he found on examination nothing at all to indicate heart disease. The nurse, duly attending, said the patient was on digitalis. As digitalis is a drug which slows the pulse, Sandy ordered the nurse to cut it out and substituted a heart stimulant.

Nurse Pickles was an intelligent woman and merely remarked that she could see the end of her enjoyable stay at Whorfdale Manor.

He told the patient that he considered she would be fit in time for the Meet next week.

'I don't know how to thank you,' she said. 'I knew you were a good doctor the moment I saw you!'

Sandy said he'd like to be present at the Meet as he had never seen one and got an immediate and cordial invitation from Milady. She looked forward to Dr Flanagan's displeasure when he could see her at the Meet.

Over the course of the next few days, he was able to induce a number of the cardiac patients to get up and walk but some had more faith in their doctor's instructions and he failed to persuade them they were now cured. So, bed-ridden they remained. Sandy conjectured that for some, this no doubt suited some personal agenda too.

Flannelfeet could talk of nothing else but the impending Meet and spent the time polishing his great boots and flip-flopping untidily about the house talking of horses, foxhounds, hot bitches, the yellows and anything connected with the stewardry of the sport. He was an authority, was Flanagan.

His wife too got busy cleaning his 'pink' coat spotless, one sleeve suitably adjusted for his plaster and ironing his breeches into the requisite shape. He had lost all interest in the practice for which Sandy was heartily glad otherwise he would have seen his rapidly diminishing visiting list.

His wife's dogs loitered around the house neglected and smelling the house out like a kennel. Sandy determined that as soon as he'd seen this Meet and the

Hunt go off, he'd be off himself, for fresher fields and any pastures new.

The great day came so he made off early in the car to Whorfdale Manor to see how the patient fared. He found her in the spacious hall, supervising the arrangement of snacks of eatables with bottles of sherry and port set invitingly on a table. A large fire was burning in the wide stone fireplace and the parquet flooring and furniture shone from the obvious efforts of her household staff.

The mullioned hall windows toned down the bright morning sun, which showed up an inscription on the wall which he noticed for the first time. It was deeply cut into the stonework and gilded as in the fashion of some gravestones. It set out the genealogical tree of the Kirby-Whorfs and was a long and highly diverting pedigree of that illustrious family, complete with by-blows and bar sinister. But the most astonishing thing, Sandy saw, was that it was headed by no less a person than Beowolf!

'Goes back a bit, doesn't it?' said an amused voice beside him. The Lady of The Manor pointed with her crop to the legend. 'Pay no attention to that nonsense!' she said with a laugh. 'My late husband was a commoner himself so he was determined to trace my family tree. He made a lot of money, making wool blankets mostly of cotton and spent some of it on this effort. Some of it is true but what he and his genealogist couldn't find, they invented and then went the whole hog and dragged in Beowolf!'

'I always thought Beowolf was a poem,' said Sandy, 'or one of those chaps that slew a fiery dragon.'

'Probably never existed,' she replied. 'Anyway, my husband didn't like his own name which was Gummidge so he took mine by deed poll. Mind you, I'm not criticizing him. He was a decent old spud and left me pretty well off, only,' she said ruefully, 'no family to carry on the noble name.' She smiled wistfully.

A tall handsome woman, she looked a picture in her smart old-fashioned riding habit, top hat and veil. She seemed much younger than her 50 years. Perhaps the digitalis and the rest had done her good after all. But he was glad he had been instrumental in her being rescued he felt from invalidism, and that she was now happily back to a vigorous life and her much-loved 'riding to hounds.'

Sandy asked her to make no complaint about his diagnosis to Dr Flanagan, at least until after he had left the district, but they both looked forward to his expression when he saw her up and doing at the Meet and looking in splendid form in that habit.

Being forthright in his thinking with no humbug himself, he was delighted to have encountered her. He was constantly refreshed by people; people like her who left an intriguing flavour of themselves in his memory or piqued his interest however briefly, in some idiosyncratic way.

By and by, they went outside and saw that several people were assembled in the courtyard. A mixed crowd. Sandy looked in vain for the Hunting Pinks of Mannings pictures. The men looked like ostlers and the women were not at all like the pictures in Moss Bros advertisements. Just sweaters and jodhpurs for the women and tweeds and top boots for the men.

At length a little group cantered into view. The leading man was strikingly attired. He wore a cutaway black coat, light breeches and glossy black top boots. He had on a shiny black topper attached to a cord on his lapel and was smoking a cigar. His face was plump with a short black moustache and bright black eyes.

'Our Master of Foxhounds, Mr. Gorbalstein,' said Milady in Sandy's ear. 'Nice chap, stockbroker, plenty of cash which he spends freely on the Hunt. Very keen!'

He glanced at her sideways to see her smiling wickedly as she surveyed the whole scene. 'Not quite what you expected, eh Doctor?' she remarked, seeing the disappointment on his face.

'No, not quite,' Sandy replied. 'Where are all the scarlet coats?'

'Too dear,' she said, 'but wait, here are a few for you. The Huntsman and whippers-in.'

Ah! This is more like it, thought Sandy as a group appeared turned out in 'Hunting Pink' and well-mounted. Some of them disappeared towards the kennels, the whippers-in he was told, where the hounds were 'giving tongue,' if he remembered the right term. Hounds don't bark like common dogs. They 'give tongue.'

Sandy looked round for Flanagan but he appeared to be late. But soon he heard a familiar sound. In the distance carried by the gentle breeze came flip-flop, flippitty-flop. Heavens! he thought, was the man running to the Meet? But as he came in sight, Sandy saw, to his inward amusement, he was riding a horse the counterpart of himself, a long rangy animal with large flat hooves of abnormal size. He flopped up to Sandy and his companion and looked aghast at his patient.

'My dee-ar Lady Kirby-Wharf! What are you doing out of bed?'

'Going hunting if there's anything to hunt and don't try to stop me,' she said gaily. 'I'm as fit as a fiddle.' Her groom brought up her horse and putting her left foot in the stirrup she mounted lightly into the saddle and turned the horse in the direction of the Master of Fox Hounds.

'Hey you!' growled Flannelfeet rudely to Sandy. 'What's the big idea?'

'The idea,' replied Sandy politely, 'is that the patient hasn't got myocarditis anymore and a day's huntin' in my considered opinion, will do her a power of good.'

'Wish you'd mind your own business,' he scowled sulkily. He seemed to forget that that was just what Sandy was doing.

To divert his attention Sandy asked if there was a likelihood of a good day's sport.

'It's all arranged. It's a bagged fox.'

'A what?' he asked.

'A bag fox. One you let out of the bag,' he said irritably as Sandy grinned up at him, highly amused at the sight of his ears sticking out aggressively on either side of his velvet hat. 'There's been a lot of destruction of foxes lately and it's unlikely a fox will be drawn so we provide the fox for ourselves,' he said sniffily.

Sandy felt he was having no end of disillusionment. First no red coats, then a Master of Fox Hounds in a cutaway black coat and cigar, and now a home-made fox! As he voiced his chagrin, Flannelfeet said testily, 'You expect too much! Things cost money! Anyway, you see that man over there with the straw in his mouth? He'll go round the back in a minute and let the cat..er..the fox out of the bag, or in this case a cardboard box, there being no bag, and off we'll go, For-r-rard! Tally ho! and all that.'

As soon as the little fox was allowed to escape by the man with the straw, the hunt moved off with the tootling of horns and the blowing of whistles, the hounds giving tongue as hounds do.

The last person to move off was Flannelfeet as his steed had gone into a slight day dream so applying his long whip, he at last got his horse to flounder off in pursuit, the pair of them looking long and attenuated as they followed the others careering away into the distance. Alas, thought Sandy, they didn't have any of the charm of the lanky Don Quixote and his beloved mare!

Once the hunt had moved off, Sandy made his way back indoors to the consolation of the drinks and snacks, or to what was left of the depredations made by the hunting fraternity. Taking a large port and a broken sandwich, he sat down by the fire.

How are the mighty fallen he sighed. He picked up a discarded copy of the Times and was deep into the Times Literary Supplement, when, not twenty minutes after he had sat down, he heard a commotion outside; more hounds giving tongue, more horns and whistles.

He got up and hurried outside to see the entire Whorfdale Hunt tearing across the courtyard at full tilt, the whole outfit disappearing around the back of the house with much view-hallooing and 'Gone awa-ay!'s.'

And here were old Flannelfeet and steed, late as usual, flip-flopping along. And a sorry sight the huntin' man looked too, leading his horse, capless, his bonny red coat plastered in mud, and very wet.

The sight of those great boots and the horse's great hooves flip-flopping towards him nearly unmanned Sandy. Tactlessly, he asked if he'd had an accident.

'Accident you fool? I've taken a toss, and damme if I didn't land in a ditch full of water! Where's that damned fox?'

'Judging by his direction,' said Sandy doing his best not to laugh at this last straw, 'I imagine he's made for his little cardboard box again.'

'Shouldn't be surprised!' he grunted glumly. 'That's the worst of a bagged fox. The blighter has no-where to go so heads back to where he came from!'

Whoosh! he sneezed loudly.

'Come on,' said Sandy, commiseratingly. 'Get rid of Rosinante and I'll drive you back home in the car. I've got a rug in the back. You'll catch your death of cold if you hang about here much longer.'

'What do you mean, Rosinate? This isn't a mare!' he said, oblivious to the allusion. 'He's called Ben Bolt,' and he slapped the rangy animal affectionately before handing him over to a groom who had materialized due to the ruckus. He gave him careful instructions as to grooming, watering and feeding. Going by the man's sardonic expression they were patently redundant.

Sandy was keen to get him home as he had no wish to carry on for him if he was taken ill. He had no desire to extend this particular locum by a day.

Toodles, as he called his wife, greeted their arrival with little shrieks of consternation and commiseration. He explained that he would never have taken a toss if his plaster splint hadn't got in the way of him controlling the trusty Ben Bolt properly.

After a hot bath and a couple of aspirins however, he pronounced himself fit again. That evening Sandy found him flip-flopping around again but this time in patent leather shoes and dinner jacket. On enquiring the reason for this grandeur, he replied that he was expecting a colleague for dinner.

'He's been up at Harrogate visiting some tart he's keen on. On his way back home to Ousel, I put him up for the night. Serves as an alibi in case his wife ever finds out. Nice chap though and making tons of dough in a multiple practice, – huge panel and private. Don't envy him though,' he continued. 'Wouldn't be seen dead in that dirty old town. Maybe he'll give you a job as a locum. I won't need you in a day or two. I think I'll give huntin' a rest and get back to the old routine. If I can't ride Ben Bolt with this wrist, I can still drive a car.'

And that's exactly what happened. Dr Scroggie of Ousel at dinner that night asked Sandy when he would be free as his senior partner in the firm was having his hæmorrhoids injected and might be off for a week or two at least.

Flanagan agreed to release him that night. Sandy smiled, probably glad to get rid of him after taking his most lucrative patient off his list! In the morning, he followed Dr Scroggie to Ousel, some fifty miles away. Dirty old town or not, he was heartily glad to be off and sorely tempted to shout 'Gone Awa-aa-ay!' as he drove off.

⏵ Chapter 13 ⏴

Nobody would describe Ousel as a beautiful city but his accommodation was lovely and couldn't have been further from old Flannelfeet's malodorous establishment. Dr Scroggie was well off enough to do himself in style.

He saw on arrival that the doctor had a fine corner house with a double drive with a well-kept lawn in front. This looked promising. Later discovery showed a large garden at the back and a garage for two cars that led onto a side street.

To his delight he found the victuals were first rate; Dr Scroggie said that he was so infernally busy that the only pleasures he had time to enjoy were good food and a comfortable home.

Mrs. Scroggie, Sandy found, was a nice little woman, well-read and a good conversationalist. But she would keep on knitting things. If it wasn't socks for her husband, it was scarves and pullovers. She knitted as she read and knitted as she talked. Scroggs, as Sandy found his partners called him, said she even knitted in bed.

'Why this passion for knitting?' he asked her one evening.

'My mother's fault,' she explained. 'She kept us girls at it all the time. Like my husband, my family were Scottish fisherfolk from up on the North East Coast and fishermen use a lot of knitted things you know – and my husband refuses to wear bought socks,' she smiled. 'I need to keep up the supply as he wears them out with that boot thing of his.'

She was referring to the doctor's club foot. He was a stocky Scot, bald, pale-faced and dogged-looking. He was strongly built and would have been handicapped by his club foot if he had not used it as a mallet to bang on the floor for emphasis and actually to accelerate his progress along the street by swinging the clumsy thing like a counterbalance. He was a man of terrific energy and assumed the bulk of the panel work.

'It suits me better than attending private patients. I've neither the time nor the patience to sit and blether and the panel patients don't expect much of that!' he told Sandy who was in some sympathy with this. He too found it rather trying.

It gave Scroggs time to do a great many visits a day. He simply tore about, and in his surgery, didn't trouble to sit down, one minute bending over his desk to scribble a panel line and the next, whizzing out to give the dispenser some instructions or to borrow a knife to incise a boil.

Sandy learned that in this practice the division of profits was according to the share bought by each partner. Since these shares were unequal, it caused much heart-burning in the bosoms of their wives. So, the wives elected not to visit each other.

'Damn good idea,' said Scroggs. 'If they don't meet, they can't fight.'

One of the partners was Pell, a Fellow of the Royal College of Surgeons. He did the surgical work in a local nursing home, subsidised by the firm, Sandy discovered.

This was in order to keep other surgeons out and so keep surgical profits in.

Like most men holding a Fellowship he felt himself a cut above his physician colleagues and flatly refused to have anything to do with panel work. The others regarded him as a nuisance, though essential, but considered he had a soft time of it; the days when the others failed to persuade anyone to have something removed, the surgeon spent his time in a shed at the back of the house, indulging in his favourite hobby of carpentry.

Sandy found this highly amusing, wondering privately, if this was how he kept his hand in. But Pell told him one day, 'I love carpentry and if I'd had my own way, I would never have become a surgeon. I much prefer operating on wood, – far rather than on human beings! The results are better and more lasting.'

The other two partners were Dr Formby, a Yorkshireman and founder of the firm, the man with the hæmorrhoids, and the other, a Dr Payne, a bright young lad from the Leeds Medical School.

A large building in the middle of the town was wholly taken up by four surgeries, four waiting rooms, two dispensaries and an office with a cash registered adding machine operated by a male book-keeper. It also had an attic occupied by the caretaker and his wife.

He learned that jealous members of the opposition sarcastically called this building the clearing house of the factory. He became aware of the reason for these opprobrious terms when he had done a day in Dr Formby's surgery.

The patients came in their dozens, old and young, children and adolescents, panel and private. The form, he discovered, was that the panel were disposed of at record speed but a little more time was spent on the private patients as each of the latter represented two and sixpence cash with tuppence on the bottle.

The tempo of the two lady dispensers agreed with the speed of the doctors, with a slight advantage, as hundreds of bottles for digestive mixtures to cough mixtures and tonics, were already made up – all from very simple ingredients, he found, – so there was little waiting. The patient handed in a slip of paper with a number on it and received in return his or her precious bottle, neatly wrapped up and sealed with sealing wax.

Sandy had a bundle of these slips before him on his desk. They were numbered 1, 1a, 2a, 2b, 3a, 3b and so on, each representing a different mixture which was considered appropriate to the malady or complaint. These were culled from a list that had to be memorized before surgery started.

After diagnosis he handed the slip to the patient who hastened off to present it to the pigeon hole in the dispensary door. The irrepressible Sandy couldn't help but regard this as somewhat comical. Not so the patient who hurried off, happy with the tonic or medicine and with complete faith in it.

The process did save a lot of time – and it needed to be saved too. Surgery started at 8am and he was still seeing patients at 10am. He began to perspire. But then, so was everyone else perspiring. Not so the surgeon, who wandered around and had a chat with whoever was willing and now and then getting underfoot.

At about 9.30 Sandy had a temporary breather, so went to have a look at the others and the man with the cash register who was ringing up his half crowns and tuppences at great speed. It was all very efficient.

Later when he had eventually finished surgery, he had to agree with the opposition's somewhat sarcastic denunciation, this was, without doubt, a clearing house.

The analogy to a factory seemed rather apt too; it was indeed commercializing medicine; little or no doctoring was being done. Anything troublesome was sent with a note to the local hospital, and any patient willing to pay who was remotely suspected of needing surgical intervention, was sent to Mr. Pell the surgeon. He learned that if that hard-working man was out, the patient was asked to return on Sunday, the day fixed for more detailed examination when things were quieter.

After the last Yorkshireman had left with his magic bottle, they all gathered in the office and Scroggs signified that it had been another highly successful day and his partners agreed.

Looking at his visiting list Sandy had a few qualms as he had 30 patients to see at their homes and he was not at all familiar with the town yet. The others went their various ways and Scroggs remained with Sandy to advise him on how to do his rounds in the fastest possible time. He handed him a street map to help him find his way by the best routes.

'I need to ask,' said Sandy. 'Do you enjoy this kind of practice?'

'No,' replied Scroggs, unequivocally. 'I hate it. It isn't medicine at all, but it's a damn good way of making money quickly. Have you any idea how much we knock down annually? Total earnings last year were seventeen thousand, five hundred quid. Good isn't it?'

Golly! thought Sandy. 'Yes, that's good alright, but what about your conscience?'

'Well,' he admitted. 'It did bother me a bit but I got caught in the current and although I often feel like pulling out, I just can't make up my mind to. I've been doing this for 15 years now and I've saved and invested a good bit of money. Made it possible to put my son into a good prep school in England and he's now in Fettes School in Edinburgh. To see Ian, you would never believe his grandfather gutted herring and sold them at 12 a penny. I intend he should specialize in Medicine. As you know he will need a deal of money to do that too. Perhaps that helps to salve my conscience, – and if *we* don't carry all these patients and supply them with their weekly bottles of the magic stuff, some other firm will.'

'But,' Sandy objected, 'don't you miss a lot of serious disease working at this speed?'

'Of course we do, but what's the remedy? There ought to be a clinic where we could send doubtful cases. The hospital is fed to the back teeth with our clearing-house methods but I don't see any way out under the present system of general practice. Anyway, we must get on. I have another 60 odd visits to do.'

And with that, away went the typical general practitioner of a busy industrial city, swinging his club foot and banging it down with a thump as if to say, no damned club foot was keeping *him* down!

As the days passed, Sandy began to get a certain kick out of the daily rush; the sensation of trying to beat the clock had something thrilling in it. Dashing about all day in and out of the car, up and down stairs and in and out of houses certainly keeps a body fit he thought. House meals were gobbled with his thoughts fixed on other patients still to do and worrying how to fit it all in.

With the clatter of feet and clinking of bottles in the dispensary, the hum of conversations with the cash register making a constant crash of sound in the background, Sandy said facetiously that all this could be made into a symphony. Scroggs said it would be more phoney than symph and suggested a good title would be *Medicos in Excelsis*!

As human beings the patients seemed not to exist, there was no intimate contact. They became simply something to be disposed of as quickly as possible so that after a few days Sandy failed to identify one from the other unless he or she had something wrong that was of sufficient singularity to claim his full attention.

It wasn't long though, before Dr Formby returned, hæmorrhoids suitably dealt with and looking very sprightly and fit in spite of his seventy years.

The firm went into a huddle and then offered Sandy an Assistantship. They'd been impressed that he was such a fast worker.

He felt this was a real compliment from these energetic medicos but knew that this was really not his idea of Medicine, so not for him.

He simply thanked them but said he had not yet found his metier so he needed to move on. Wishing them continuing success he set off back to London and the Medical Agency for another position.

▶ Chapter 14 ◀

Although the peripatetic life of a locum suited him, he couldn't help but give the paucity of funds some thought as he left the lucrative Ousel firm behind and motored south.

Inevitably larger financial reward was of some interest, especially as he got older. Regrettably this was barely forthcoming as a locum. He was now past 40 and he really did like his creature comforts. It had taken him quite a while to be able to afford his small second-hand car, but a car certainly gave him more scope to keep him in work.

Yet Dr Scroggie and Co's life was, he felt, not only far from his idea of doctoring but neither the way he wished to accrue significant funds towards settling down, so earning enough for his own practice was certainly not in the offing at any point he could see.

His innate restlessness, that same quirk that had set him off at the first opportunity at 21 away from the gentle rather proscribed life of his parents, had led to his early venturing and adventuring in the West Indies. Even the 'on-the-edge-of-life' of those four grim, brutal years in France and Belgium had in its horrible way been accommodated by this aspect of his character, this restless spirit. It might even have exacerbated it; it had certainly unsettled him. Somehow there was always that spur of independence.

His parents' sporadic admonitions to him to settle down came to mind as he drove along. They did make him wonder if he ever would. Or could for that matter, he thought with a chuckle. How this ideal was to materialize was somewhat shrouded in the mists of conjecture and mostly he felt, impossibility. It was in any case a moot question.

As he entered the outskirts of London once more, he thought wryly that there were always a few stints in the West African Medical Service for some extra dough if one was game enough to try.

* * *

Back in Town, he was lucky enough to get another position straight away; the doctor was recovering from an attack of pneumonia so needed a locum.

The doctor and his wife had two sets of twins aged two and four. The wife kept an incredibly untidy house with the doubtful help of a slatternly maid. Meals were sketchy and not improved by the yelling and largely unrestrained behaviour of the twins at the table.

Sandy really could not tolerate this so made it plain that he would have to go if something wasn't done. Thereafter he was greatly relieved by the children having their meals in the kitchen with the maid. The hullabaloo from the four small children, who seemed to have excellent lungs, was now somewhat diminished and so fairly tolerable.

It was evident that the wife had no idea of running a house. The food was always badly cooked, fried chops with soggy greens which looked as bad as they tasted. He felt it was no wonder the busy working doctor was ill having to subsist on such a diet.

In the evenings, Sandy was puzzled by the fact that between 9 and 10pm, the wife would dash off in her car, returning about half an hour later, looking extremely happy. At first he thought perhaps she had a lover, but then he caught a whiff of a certain aroma and suddenly said aloud, 'I know what it is! It's chips!'

'Wh-at!' she cried blushing crimson and looking guilty.

'Come on now,' said Sandy laughing. 'Confess! You have a weakness for chips. It's nothing to be ashamed of!'

'Yes,' she admitted. 'It's chips. As you know, I have the best of meals in my own home but I have a passion for fish and chips from the chip shop and eaten all smoking hot out of the paper with salt and vinegar. Blimey,' she said lapsing into the vernacular in her enthusiasm. 'They do taste good where I buy'em. Before I met my husband, I used to work in a shop in Camden Town and every night when we finished me and my pal used to make right for the chipper and have a proper feast. My husband doesn't know though he sometimes remarks about the smell. He wouldn't half be affronted if he found out, so don't you tell him.'

'Wouldn't dream of it!' he replied, smiling.

'Ooh!' she sighed happily, 'I take the Ford down to Camden Town to the same chipper and park in a side street and eat my paperful there. D'you know, I can't get out of the habit. It doesn't matter how nice a meal I have at home, I must have my chips.'

Thinking of the ghastly food she actually dished up he wasn't at all surprised. But chips were definitely not his fare.

One night after a visit to the pictures and a decent meal, Sandy was on a bus going up the Camden Rd. Just as it was slowing down for the bus stop at Carraras Tobacco factory, he saw a slight figure dash across to the bus stop. Suddenly out of no-where, a car, coming up at great speed from the Hampstead Road merely tapped that slight figure with the right wing of the car and shot him right under the front wheels of the bus. Sandy distinctly heard a hollow pop and crunch as the off-side wheel hit the skull.

Feeling sick and most disinclined to get out and attend to the body, he made his way outside, dreading what he might see and knowing he must do what he could and to shield the body till the police and ambulance arrived. There was the driver to see to as well who was bound to be in a state of shock. There was no choice. He was a doctor.

He found out later that the man was a young Cypriot and the driver of the car was being chased by a police car after a smash and grab raid in the West End.

Yes, he hated street accidents.

He was glad that he was able to leave this particular locum shortly afterwards. Naturally he never told her husband about his wife's illicit passion and presumed she was still indulging her taste at the chipper in Camden Town every night.

Sandy's next locum was surprisingly short-lived. This time he was sent to the Elephant and Castle district. There he was dismayed to discover that at least 50% of his patients had gastric or duodenal ulcers, gastritis and dyspepsia. The local appetite was for chips, chips and more chips – highly recommended for men, women and children by no less a person than Lord Woolton, he discovered. And the favourite fare of the soldiers and sailors on leave too.

Sandy fought a losing battle; any and all advice on a better diet he found was quite lost on his ailing patients. It fell on the stoniest of stony ground. No-one seemed interested in the fate of their digestive system.

As always, he grumbled to himself, it was left to the doctor to do what he could with the results.

Unfortunately for Sandy it wasn't long before he himself fell foul of gastro-enteritis and nearly perished as a result of it. Not a happy locum by any means.

Once recovered but somewhat peely-wally, he blessed his luck by being offered a locum in Weymouth. It was summertime and since his duties turned out to be far less onerous than most locums, he had enough off-duty to spend time on the sandy beach in his swim trunks lying on a rug or swimming in the sea or boating. In a month he had acquired a tan as good as the one he had in Barbados as a young man revelling in those exotic tropics.

By the time he was back seeking his next locum, he had thankfully fully regained his usual health and vigour and was ready to see what next was on offer.

◗ **Chapter 15** ◖

Because he invariably lived in the doctor's house while doing his stint as a locum, the doctor's wife played a considerable part in his stay while he filled in for the medico he was sent to relieve. She was after all the source of his meals and the state of the domestic arrangements. And naturally Sandy took a keen interest in these. Experience and a dash of Scots pessimism however, meant his expectations of them were always on the low side.

He had accepted a locum in a town well-known for its educational facilities and its architectural beauty which pleased him very much, used as he was to the grimier parts of London and his stints in places like Ousel and other such towns in the North and Midlands.

It was evening when he arrived at the house, and he was met by the doctor himself, a short grey-haired man in his fifties, who, in a rather thick voice apologized for the non-appearance of his wife; she was in bed with a headache and to dump his bags in the hall.

He led the way to the dining room and in an apologetic voice, indicated Sandy's dinner. On a plate with a knife and fork sat an enormous veal and ham pie, sufficient Sandy thought for six people at least. He eyed its lonely state with some disfavour.

'No maid, no dinner, wife gone to bed,' the Doctor muttered throatily. 'What'll you drink? I've plenty of that anyway,' and opened a sideboard to reveal a goodly stock of gin, whisky and bottles of beer.

'I'll have a whisky and soda thank you,' said Sandy gratefully, thinking of that unadorned pie.

'Good, my taste exactly. Sit down and help yourself,' he replied pointing to the veal and ham monstrosity.

He did so and offered some to the doctor who declined. He seated himself opposite Sandy with his well-charged glass and after taking stock of his new locum with his protuberant and blood-shot eyes, said,

'Like music?'

'Very much,' Sandy replied.

'Classical?'

'Yes,' agreed Sandy, 'Classical.'

'Right. There's some Wagner at the Prom tonight. I'll switch it on.' Staggering slightly, he made for the room opposite where he turned the radio on full blast.

'What about disturbing your wife?' asked Sandy rather anxiously.

'She's alright. Tell you about her in a minute.'

Having recharged their glasses with a generous amount of whisky and a mere dash of soda, he then proceeded to regale Sandy with what he obviously longed to get off his chest including the events of the past 24 hours.

He first asked if he was married. No, he was not married.

'Take Punch's advice! Don't! This is my second, a fair terror. Squanders my earnings like water and abuses me as well. My first was a quiet economical woman but she died five years ago of carcinoma. I fell in with this one and my life has been a fair hell since. Her name's Vera – damned silly name. We've two kids, Jackie and Blanche. Jackie's four, Blanche two. Jackie has infantile eczema poor little blighter and goes around swathed in bandages. Can't cure it, tried everything. Well, Vera's idea was to have a holiday as far away from me as possible. Right-o says I, suits me and I book a house I see advertised as furnished at a delectable sea-side resort and packed her and the kids off early this morning. Although the place is 80 odd miles away, she insisted on going by taxi, – she can't take Jackie on the train she said. Gets fed up explaining the bandages, 'Has the little boy had an accident?' and other footling questions. Well, judge my surprise,' continued the doctor, 'half an hour before you arrived, there's the taxi outside with the whole gang back here again! 'What's the big idea?' I asked. She bawled at me and called me a fool for booking the house by phone without ever seeing it. She said it was practically a ruin, rickety beds, no sanitation. Took one look and came right back. 'What do you intend to do now?' I asked. 'Do?' she said. 'I'm going to bed – you square the taxi.' I reminded her that I was expecting a locum. 'Give him some of that pie then and some of your drink if you can spare it,' she said. 'That'll do for him. If he's like your other locums, he'll be an expert in elbow-bending!' and with that she went off to bed with two cups of tea and three aspirins. Rude, ain't she? What a life, eh? Let's have another drink!'

There was nothing useful Sandy could say but the doctor didn't seem to expect any response for he moved to the lounge and switched off the radio. Wagner had ended and there was only an unpleasant cacophony blaring from it.

'Well,' said Sandy. 'I think I'll turn in now Dr Weir, if I'm to work tomorrow.'

'No, no,' he said. 'Don't worry about work. There's practically nothing to do. Sit down and we'll have a yarn.'

It seemed obvious Dr Weir meant to make it a session and as it was his responsibility, Sandy acquiesced.

He was obviously glad of the company and the conversation between the two of them was varied and interesting; some subjects grave, some amusing. This included medicine, music and lastly, the female of the species.

Throughout though, Dr Weir preferred to stand to his refreshment with one foot on the kerb of the fireplace and one elbow leaning negligently on the mantel. After a while however, his elbow was inclined to slip and in spite of Sandy suggesting he sit down, he steadfastly refused to do so.

It must have been well after midnight when the lounge door was suddenly thrust open and Sandy was astonished to see a very attractive young woman in her night attire standing in the doorway. She was clearly in a towering rage.

Ignoring Sandy, she snarled, 'Idiot! You're drunk again!'

Dr Weir's elbow skidded the length of the mantelpiece and he collapsed face down onto the carpet, knocking over a small table and a large vase of flowers which joined him on the floor. The young woman quickly stepped forward and poured what was left of the water in the vase over the defenceless head of her husband. It failed to rouse him.

In some confusion Sandy offered to help the doctor up to bed.

'Please go,' she said resignedly. 'I can manage my husband best on my own. I'm used to this. You'll find your room – I've left the door open. I don't suppose the old fool showed you. Your bags are still in the hall,' she added dismissively, glaring grimly down at her husband lying damply at her feet.

Sandy beat a hasty retreat. Some hours later he was awakened by unsteady footsteps on the landing. He guessed she had actually left him to sleep it off on the floor and only now was the poor doctor able to make his way to bed.

The following morning, the doctor did not appear which didn't really surprise him. Mrs. Weir however, looking remarkably fresh, produced a marvelous breakfast. They both sat down to it and both of them did it full justice.

'It's a relief to see a man enjoy his food as you do Dr MacNeil. Donald usually has such a hangover that he can't look at food until lunchtime and then only after sundry Gin and bitters,' she remarked, a slight edge to her voice. 'I've got the visiting list made up,' she added in a different and friendly tone, 'and if you care to set off immediately after the 9 o' clock surgery, you might be finished by lunchtime and have the afternoon free. If you like, you can drive me up to town as I have some shopping to do and a maid to engage. I'll show you the town, or what there is of it.

This was so charmingly said that he found it hard to reconcile it with the virago of their first encounter. She made no reference at all to the events of the night before and Sandy certainly had no wish to. He began to wonder what made the doctor go off on the binge like that? Dipsomania perhaps? But later in the day, he thought he might have found the answer.

The child Jackie, was a thin, alert and bright boy, the type Sandy had found previously in children with the condition that so badly affected this little four year old. He had an unrelieved eczema of face, arms and legs. His legs and arms were bandaged to stop him scratching and the thin little face was badly blemished by the eruption and wore the worried look associated with this malady. He could see readily what a worry this was when nothing had been found to alleviate it.

Coming back to lunch, he found Dr Wier armed with a bottle of Dry Gin and one of Angostura bitters. It was obvious already that he had been enjoying himself with several pink gins before Sandy's return, judging by his heightened colour and look of satisfaction. He accepted a cocktail as the doctor explained that his wife never took alcohol as it upset her.

The lunch was as good as the breakfast; he still couldn't understand Weir's grievance against her. In the afternoon, he took her shopping in the car as she had suggested and looked around the town. But he found himself more interested in his companion. She seemed a different woman, so happy and friendly.

'I'm glad you're a locum who isn't a bloated old booze-hound,' she said. 'Though I notice you like a drink. Perhaps in another ten years, you'll be just like other locums.'

'I agree,' said Sandy with a laugh. 'I'm tending that way! But if I can drag myself away from this fascinating mode of living, there's no knowing, I might take up a practice on my own account one day.'

'Fascinating? Do you mean to say, you *like* being a locum?'

'Yes, now I have evolved a technique for dealing with doctors' wives.'

'The Casanova approach?'

'Not a bit of it! I'm just more able to persuade my unwilling hostesses to treat me reasonably even though I am 'only the locum' especially where food is concerned. And I do get an inexpressible delight in observing my fellow man and his mate and their reactions to life, and marriage come to that. – 'I'm a cheil amang ye, takin' notes,' to quote Robbie Burns!'

'Thanks for the warning,' Vera replied laughing, 'I'll watch my step from now on!'

As they drove home, he was able to add to his impression of her. He'd already noted that a hairdresser had something to do with her blonde hair. And although she was pretty, her well-shaped mouth as well as her eyes had a hardness about them. Now he felt that despite the smiling demeanour, she was a very angry young woman underneath.

When they got back to the house, they found the doctor seated by the fire in the lounge, hunched untidily over a steaming cup of tea. He was obviously enjoying it going by his sighs of pleasure. His nose was very red and his gray hair was all over the place.

'Crikey! Beauty unadorned!' cried Vera scornfully but obviously finding the sight amusing.

Donald looked up and said glumly, 'I suppose you've been trying to ruin me. Are you aware that my current account is overdrawn?'

'Overdrawn!' retorted his wife. 'It's your liquor account that's overdrawn! By the way I've decided to book rooms at a hotel for a holiday with the children. I want a change from cooking and housekeeping. I'm going to Bournemouth.'

'Nice inexpensive place,' growled the doctor. 'I have also decided on my holiday. I intend to tour the Cathedrals of England. I have always wanted to tour the Cathedrals of England and now I'm going to do it, come what may!'

'You mean the pubs of England and I can prophesy what'll come of it, – the D.T.'s.' laughed Vera mockingly over her shoulder as she left the room.

The following day she set off with the children, this time seen off on the train by Dr Weir and Sandy. As they drove home, the doctor said, 'Thank the Lord that damned nuisance is gone. Now we can enjoy a few nights of real music.'

'What? Aren't you going on your tour?' asked a puzzled Sandy.

'All in good time. All in good time! I can now settle down to some serious drinking and solace my starved soul with music!'

'Do you mean you have no intention of doing the Cathedrals?'

'Far from it! I have every intention but for the next week at least I am going to exercise my musical emotions and indulge my physical being in things that are normally forbidden. Your job is to keep up the illusion that I'm away on my holiday. By the way, there's some horrible old woman coming in as a daily to 'do' for us so if the cuisine isn't up to the mark, try and stick it till Vera comes back.'

Fortunately, Dr Weir tired early of his Booze and Bach parties and in a couple of days set out on his Cathedral tour. He went off in great glee with one small suitcase and a bottle of Scotch with a dozen Bass in the back seat of his big Austin, leaving Sandy with the affairs of the practice.

Happy to do so, he settled down to do a limited number of visits which left him much spare time to spend exploring the surrounding countryside, reading and catching up on his correspondence.

A week had drifted pleasantly by, when a phone message from Mrs. Weir said she was coming home and bringing a promising domestic with her.

Well, thought Sandy, this isn't as bad as Dr Weir coming back, not least for the liver and nervous system. He imagined his routine would remain the same and the cooking greatly improve.

When she returned, the children were mostly kept out from underfoot in the garden or with the maid. Mrs. Weir had not enjoyed the seaside resort; not a decent man in sight, just a lot of old bores and tea hounds. She invited Sandy to the pictures and the odd drive out teasing Sandy on what she called his obsession with food.

'If you had lived in as many doctor's houses as I have, you'd develop an obsession with food!' he retorted, and went on to describe details of the cooking he'd endured. 'A locum needs the digestion of the proverbial ostrich!' he laughed. 'and only the pace at which I always work has saved me from fatty degeneration of the heart by burning off all the fried food!'

Commiserating with him she was then kindness itself and took some pains with Sandy's meals and general comfort. Harmony being the result she talked quite freely about her background, her German origins, and her upbringing in England. Her father taught music and had lived in this country for many years.

Sandy was quite unsuspecting that she had an ulterior motive in this. Being always interested in people and naturally lives that differed somewhat from his own, he was a natural listener.

She told him of a Franz Bohr she had met as a very young woman while he was in England consulting a bone specialist over a severe foot problem. This was the result he'd said of underfeeding in Germany during the blockade of 1918. They'd met at a promenade concert and she took him home to meet her family. They'd fallen in love but Papa was very against it. He believed the bone was tubercular and made Franz a very poor prospect as a husband and for fathering children, so put his foot down. She accepted this dictum and Franz returned to Heidelberg to finish his studies at University. That then was the end of that. But Franz was now back in England, in fact had been getting treatment for over a year.

She had now been seeing him for nearly a year and Dr Weir had discovered their association.

'Instead of being sensible about it,' she complained, 'he was quite intolerably jealous! and really hated Franzie. He did allow him to come to the house a few times but he couldn't get on with him – mostly because he was German,' she said. 'He told me to 'keep that bloody German away from the house!' The result was that she went on seeing Franz clandestinely. 'What else could we do?' she asked.

Then Vera dropped her bombshell.

She longed to meet Franz in comfort instead of their usual hole-in-the-corner assignations. Would Sandy mind if she had Franzie to the house?

He replied that it was her house and she could do as she pleased. Also, he was no tale-bearer, but it really was a bit thick to say the least. Was that why Donald was hitting the drink so hard? he asked. She said it might be so, but he was always pretty fond of the drink in any case.

Sandy sympathies were with the doctor but he was only the locum; it was neither his house nor responsibility. It also transpired that Franz and his father were somewhat sympathetic to the National Socialist Party in Germany, and this Donald had *not* liked. No wonder he'd cast him forth. But Sandy, as always intrigued to meet people with vastly different lives and also being perfectly happy to brush up on his German, said, 'Yes, Okay.'

Franz then became a frequent visitor, always in the evening as his treatment took up most of his day. Much to Vera's disgust he and Sandy found much to interest the pair of them.

In fact, Sandy found him very agreeable. His medical eye however, naturally noted his pallor. This actually made his typical and usual dueling scar down one cheek quite prominent. Franz was very proud of this and entertained Sandy with how he had acquired it. He was also a thoughtful but ardent supporter of the new political situation in Germany. Sandy was not particularly interested to hear about these views; he liked Franz as a plain student of Heidelberg and told him that his own Scottish University was long affiliated with Heidelberg and had the same Student Varsity song, 'Gaudemus Igatur.'

The pair of them enjoyed themselves hugely in playing the piano and lustily singing jolly German songs. Franz asked Sandy how he had learnt German, so told him; from a dear old German Jew, Gustav Hein. Franz frowned at that and asked if he was still alive.

'No,' said Sandy. 'In 1914 during the propaganda about Belgian atrocities the good citizens of my native town hounded poor Gustav to death. He lost his job as a teacher, they took away his pension and shoved him into the workhouse where he died. I think they had some idiotic idea he was a spy.'

Sandy saw to it that he and Franz spent a lot of time talking, arguing, singing and drinking beer, but it became all too plain to a seething Vera that Sandy was playing a game. Alas for her, most of their conversation was in German of which she had only a smattering. This made her feel even more excluded. Worse still, Sandy saw to it that Franzie was either too full of unaccustomed English beer, or it was too late for him to go off with Vera for the anticipated love-making. As he was not sport enough to go off and leave them, she was no better off than before.

'Look here!' said Vera fiercely, one night when Franz had gone off narrowly missing his train. 'I want a word with you! I know your game! You keep him amused until

Donald's return with your singing and silly yarns so I don't get a chance to enjoy myself!' She was fairly boiling with rage.

'Yes,' he agreed. 'That is the idea. It's a pity, but he does seem to like my company.'

'You swine!' she burst out. 'I'll tell Franz what you've been up to and he'll never speak to you again!'

Alas for poor Vera, Franz was obviously stronger mentally than physically and implied to Sandy that he was relieved and rather glad of the excuse.

A couple of days later, just before Franz's nightly arrival, they were at dinner when the phone rang. Sandy went to answer it to hear Dr Weir on the other end. He made some fatuous remark and asked for his wife. She got up with a grimace and took the phone from him. Sandy could hear him plainly as he greeted her.

'Hello dearie. Gone to bed with the Nazi yet?'

'If you can't talk sense,' Vera replied, in a virtuous voice, 'I shall hang up. Are you drunk again?'

'Not yet, but I'm on my way to it!' he laughed raucously. 'How are things? Are we bankrupt yet?'

'Now I know you're drunk,' she retorted. 'All I know is that the practice has improved since you left and the house smells less like a brewery.'

'Now listen dearest wife, I've seen plenty of Cathedrals and moreover I don't trust you so I'm coming home tomorrow, that's all, goodbye.'

'Well, try your best to get under the wheels of a bus,' said the exasperated Vera, 'and if you do ring again, do so before the *Cathedrals* are open! Good*bye*!'

She sat down at the table and burst into tears. 'See what you've done, you rotten locum you! You've ruined my life. The entire week gone and no chance to be alone with Franz. How can you be so mean?'

She looked so pathetic that Sandy felt really remorseful. 'Alright, alright, I'll bury my scruples. I'll go out soon, to the pictures or somewhere and I won't be back till all hours.'

'Thank you,' she said softly and smiled damply at him. Knowing his weakness for port she got up and poured him one to the brim, then had one herself.

He had anticipated a quick release from this locum but he was doomed to disappointment. On his return the doctor said No, he didn't feel like work just yet and had a week's drinking to do before he could face up to the winter. So out came the bottles again and Mozart and Beethoven filled the house with music at full blast.

'How long does this sort of thing go on?' Sandy asked Vera, well into yet another week.

'Oh, one day he'll wake up sober the phase having passed,' she said a little resignedly. 'You'll get your cheque and he'll be on the water wagon for another few months. I never know, – but it could happen any day.'

'But what about the reaction?' asked Sandy in some concern. 'Won't he be difficult to live with?'

'Not at all,' she said. 'He'll dope himself up with barbiturates, or a noggin or two of tincture of opium and be as good as gold – as long as you don't tell him about Franz,' she warned.

'No, I told you I was no tale-bearer,' replied Sandy, hoping this state of affairs would clear up pretty soon. But at least the practice was humming along alright in his care and as locum's go, not too arduous.

The next half day, Vera suggested that the two men take Jackie off to Whipsnade Zoo for a treat. Sandy readily agreed, though he had a good idea of Vera's plans. The doctor looked glum until Sandy told him it was licensed. This cheered him up considerably and they set off with Jackie swathed in fresh bandages and looking for all the world like a severe casualty.

They motored down, and on the way, coming into Wallington, Jackie, and for that matter Dr Weir and Sandy, were diverted by the novel sight of a bunch of gliding enthusiasts being obviously enthusiastic. It was a bright breezy day and the great yellow birds were piloted by both young men and girls. They were taking what appeared to Sandy as frightful risks as they floated silently in one direction, then turning swiftly, flew back with the air current in the opposite direction. The repetitive back and forth soon palled on the two docs however, as the gliders didn't seem to be getting anywhere. No doubt, they thought, being young, they got a thrill out of it.

At Whipsnade, they parked and trailed wee Jackie to see the lions and bears and monkeys, but he was soon tired and thirsty and demanded ice-cream and cola. The thought of drink stimulated a flagging Dr Weir and a Whipsnade tram took them quickly to the catering department.

Jackie was dumped at a table with his mixture and the two men went off to the bar. They ordered two large drams to fortify themselves and chose a table where they could watch Master Jackie.

After the soothing influence of a couple of drams they got deep into an interesting medical discussion about Beethoven's deafness. After three, they were nearly reduced to tears as Sandy drew a vivid picture of the deaf musician sticking his head into the bowels of his piano in an effort to hear something of his magnificent chords and finally in despair bursting out of the house, to the dismay of his landlady, and trudging off into the pouring rain and thunder, bareheaded, his mind, no doubt, fired with mighty melodies. From this moving tale they rapidly passed on to poor Shubert dying of typhus from a louse bite, commiserating that they could have saved him nowadays. Sandy then remarked 'Well, he might have been killed by a bus or a bullet!' but before Dr Weir could answer, Sandy cried. 'Golly! Jackie's gone!'

'Wha-at! bellowed the doctor, galvanized out of his torpor, gazing wildly at where Jackie was supposedly sitting. They rapidly scanned all horizons, but no Jackie.

Some hundred yards away, not far from an elephant lumbering along with a load of kids on its back, Sandy espied a little group milling around a tall policeman.

'Bet that's him!' he cried and they careered off, red with anxiety and scotch, in that direction. Sure enough, there was a howling Jackie, his bandages hanging off like loosened puttees exposing his poor little red excoriated legs. The policeman, ignoring the voluable sympathisers, was, as befitted an officer of the law, solemnly writing in his little notebook.

'Hi!' shouted the doctor rushing forward, and snatching up his son, cried, 'It's alright! He's *my* boy!' and charged off at great speed, trailing Jackie's bandages behind him followed by Sandy and showers of abuse from the assembled onlookers.

Sandy found the sight irresistibly funny as he followed in his wake back to the tables.

They arrived, somewhat heated and breathless. They decided they'd better call it a day, enough was enough. But first poor Jackie's bandages. These were now sadly dirty and mud-stained, but they adjusted them as best they could, one to each leg, Jackie hiccupping and sniffing dolefully throughout.

As they were getting into the car his father said, 'Now look here Jackie, don't you tell Mummy.'

Jackie looked sulky. 'Yes I will! I'll tell Mummy you went into a bar and never gave me a ride on the elefun'.

'If you do,' said his harassed father, 'I won't buy you any more ice-cream and cola.'

'Don't want any ice cream and cola! I want chips!'

'Chips make you itch more, you know that.'

'Don't care,' argued Jackie. 'I want chips!'

So, chips he had while they stopped the car and visited another tavern to bolster the doctor's flagging courage as he thought of the hell he was to get if Jackie blew the gaff.

And Jackie did blow the gaff. Then Vera blew them up for a pair of useless drunken Scotchmen in bitter and highly defamatory terms.

'Scotsmen,' pleaded Sandy.

'No! Scotchmen!' she snarled, eyes blazing, 'and after I put the poor little lamb to bed, I am going out, so you two can amuse yourselves in your own uncivilized fashion.'

'Thank Heaven and Whipsnade for that,' sighed the doctor, when Vera had gone out. They had assumed their usual evening attitude in two armchairs and two scotches with the radio on, thankfully quietly, till the doctor found a suitable programme.

'I'll bet she's gone off to meet her Nazi friend,' he said.

A trifle startled, Sandy stayed silent.

'Don't worry,' said the doctor, 'I know Herr Bohm has been here. I found a half-empty packet of those vile Brazilian cigarettes he affects, and furthermore, I saw in the pantry too many beer bottles for you to have accounted for on your own.'

Sandy admitted his deductions were correct and then explained his subterfuges to keep the German amused. Donald then laughed out loud at this and said Sandy was a damned good fellow and he'd put a further fiver on his cheque.

Sandy was somewhat relieved the following morning to find the doctor in his right mind and announcing that he was now on the water wagon and ready to resume work. His misadventure with wee Jackie, he surmised, had done the trick and sobered him.

As he handed Sandy his cheque with the promised added fiver and said farewell, Sandy suggested he read the morning paper. 'Herr Bohm and all his other colleagues will soon be on the way back to the Fatherland the way Hitler is going on.'

'If he does,' said Dr Weir, 'I'll go on the water wagon for – well – anyway – a long time!'

▶ Chapter 16 ◀

After his stint with the Weirs, Sandy was again wondering where all this was getting him. Not a practice of his own, that's for sure he thought. Where on earth was the money to come from? On his return to the Medical Agency, he sat in line viewing with distaste its horrible and depressing brown and cream paint and waited with the rest of the hopeful locums to get yet another position.

Being on the permanent list naturally he did pick up a variety of locums readily enough. Although he enjoyed his work as a doctor and the constantly changing faces and personalities the monetary side however, was not really matching up to the effort. Once again, his thoughts turned to the Colonial Service in West Africa where Willie McInnes had done so well on his very first tour.

Deciding that it was at least worth a try, Sandy signed his name on the dotted line and embarked for the Gold Coast for a hopefully lucrative stint with the West African Medical Service.

He thoroughly enjoyed the sea voyage and arrived fit, refreshed and full of anticipation.

In Cracra, the capital, he was lucky enough to be immediately allocated an established practice that had just come vacant. It was out in the suburbs, though the bush was hard on the fringes nevertheless.

The unfortunate doctor in charge of it had unexpectedly and suddenly died. Apparently, he was just entering his bungalow and crumpled and fell in the doorway. His poor wife, rushing to his aid found him lying there but with no signs of life. He'd had a fatal coronary at age 56.

Thus, an experienced doctor was needed straight away. The bungalow was now vacant and the doctor's wife with a friend pending the changes in her life so Sandy was able to take possession.

It was sturdily built of stone and wood and he found to his relief that it was clean and airy. Although a little sparse the furniture was comfortable and decent. He was quite happy with the feeling of space and it was cooler that way anyway. He was glad to see there were jalousies at the windows. These were covered with copper netting against mosquitos and other insects, and the netting for the bed was of good quality – one thing he was sure of was to be assiduous in taking his regular 5 grains of quinine. Best of all there was a large fridgidaire, a Berkerfeld filter for his water and electric fans.

He'd been told that the previous doctor's houseboy had made off, frightened by the doctor's sudden death on the doorstep. This he took to be a very bad omen indeed for the house. But another houseboy had been found for him.

Settled in, Sandy soon found his hands full of a whole new world of native diseases; craw-craw, yaws, tropical ulcers, guinea worm, leprosy, among others with hideous names and symptoms. And that syphilis and elephantiasis were also prevalent among the native population. He'd done a lot of reading up on as much tropical medicine as he could on the boat coming over, but it was a far cry from seeing them in the pages of various medical publications to actually seeing them in the flesh. Human flesh and its attendant pain and suffering. Of course, added to these were a variety of insect and snake bites and even poisons from plants. There was much to learn. But Sandy was always avid to learn and found these vastly different diseases and conditions fascinating to his medical mind and skills. Of course, the totally different approach needed satisfied his constant curiosity and interest in anything new too.

His houseboy intrigued him. He was a good worker, always polite and biddable, but Sandy was puzzled by the fact that he never smiled, except very briefly with his lips closed. So used to the happy wide-mouthed smiles of the Africans he felt that this was indeed unusual.

Naturally Sandy's ever-ready curiosity made him broach the subject. The young man hung his head and seemed reluctant to answer. Now he felt he really needed to know. After some coaxing, he told Sandy his teeth were filed and he was so ashamed that he always kept his mouth closed as much as possible.

In some astonishment Sandy asked him why they were filed? 'Sorry Massa, my tribe are cannibals,' he said. He then went on to assure Sandy that he was not a cannibal now. He had left his tribe and come to the city to learn modern things and earn money. But the tribe were only cannibal he said when food sources, especially meat were poor. Only then did they send out a raiding party to get some young meat and only from tribes that were enemies or troublesome, 'so not all the time Massa.'

Well! he thought, this is Africa alright. Of course, there was no way that Sandy was not going to ask the question, 'What does human flesh taste like?' 'Like your mutton, Massa.' he answered, knowing this from the meat that suited the colonial palate and the liking for mutton chops. Sandy was of course highly diverted by all this and told him not to give it another thought. But the houseboy continued to be sure he didn't reveal his teeth.

As regards his food, he did find it took a while to accustom himself to such native foods as fu-fu, okra, plantain and avocado, but he did draw the line at the predilection for being served so much food fried in palm oil. But, on the whole, his living arrangements were perfectly amenable and, in many respects, much better than in many locums he'd done in England.

Mindful of the sad tale of Willie McInnes and the pitfalls over accruing money other than from his salary, Sandy, with true Scots caution was very careful when the opportunities availed themselves for some private surgery for the small ops he was often requested to do.

Luckily, he had honed his suturing skills in London's East End attending knife and razor attacks and was very fast and neat. This impressed his native patients no end, deep cuts and slashes being quite frequent injuries from the settling of private disputes.

He'd already made discrete enquiries of the West African Audit department. This kept a rigorous eye on all and any employees who might and did, augment their income by pure swindling, robbery, bribery and other corruption to which they were decidedly prone or on white chaps selling government mahogany on the quiet or furnishing their bungalows illegally with government surplus. The Deputy Director of Medical Services, who Sandy discovered sported a monocle and lived in very nice quarters in the lovely capital town was a keen hunter-out of any such villainy.

Of course, there were private patients with the practice and others available among the colonial population who were quite happy to have a good-looking, amusing and experienced doctor in attendance. Among these gentry there were always call-outs to the various assaults on the digestive tract and liver from overindulgence in food and, he found, a great deal of alcohol.

Then again, the European body in those alien conditions succumbed easily to what the tropical environment had to offer too. These aside from midwifery, accidents, fractures and the hundred and one things that occur in any urban practice, especially tropical.

There was also the social life, but Sandy had had a taste of that as a young man in Barbados and was not enamoured of it. Though the ladies eyed his fair hair, brighter now in the African sun, and hazel eyes with appreciation.

He was soon introduced to a fellow doctor, one Dr Clarence Gooch-Brown, 'fine, big, upstanding chap, no end of a good dancer, first-class cricketer, all round sportsman in fact, such an asset! Even plays a reasonable hand of bridge. Indispensable fellow socially!' but who disliked getting a needle into a vein and found it 'a dashed difficult job' and scorned going into the bush to the unwashed or direputable, no doubt fearful for his highly polished shoes and saved himself for his private patients at all costs. Such types were anathema to Sandy. They cast a very poor shadow as far as he was concerned and obscured those who just got on with the job.

The inescapable impression Sandy had, was that those outside this priviledged circle were merely lesser mortals and most of them considered very low indeed. No, not Sandy's cup of tea but he made sufficient appearances to satisfy the general expectations of the local luminaries and to keep his private patients happy. But there were some big social events and dances in Cracra to enliven things, and he had to have some social life. Nevertheless, it was useful having the ready excuse of being busy.

But his preferences had always been the outsider, the eccentric and those of wide and varied interests and experiences especially those quite unknown to him.

One day, having just cleaned out and packed a native patient's wound from a neglected snake bite, he was called out to an English chap who had taken a bad fall. And discovered an old soak, Pat Rumfield; he'd tripped head first off his rickety verandah, too much the worse for drink and struck his head. Scalps bleed profusely so the copious amount of blood had seriously frightened his houseboy who had fortunately run for help rather than just run away.

Attending to the scalp wound, he'd also seen that the old reprobate had a couple of incipient tropical ulcers on his scrawny legs, on view from his having been trouserless when he fell down. Sandy warned him they needed attention before they started eroding in earnest. Reluctantly Rumfield allowed him to attend to them grumbling that he didn't want any doctor poking him about and expecting to be paid; he physicked himself and had been for years. Sandy ignored this and said he'd be back.

He was happy to do this, partly through wanting to deal with those ulcers but also because the man amused him. He lived on the edge of the bush as he hated towns but had ended up in this dilapidated wooden shack that was all he had left to call his own after 40 years trading in anything he could buy and sell; his home out in the bush to which he'd been only an intermittent visitor anyway had fallen down and been partly consumed by the vegetation and insect life. He simply moved into this place just outside of town as being one of his past dropping-in places simply because he was too lazy to repair the other.

Of course, he found in Sandy an interested and keenly amused listener to his yarns of his very chequered life. The 40 years he'd spent on the West Coast of Africa were practically engraved on his phiz. His face was like brown leather stretched over his facial bones, deeply lined with permanently bloodshot black eyes set in dark cavernous orbits in a yellowish skull. His grizzled hair was tufty and quite sparce. Sandy presumed it was alopæcia but Pat assured him that, no, – this was due to a habit he had of falling asleep on the floor of his hut when drunk and in the morning being awakened by the goats chewing his hair. This seemed to disturb him not at all!

He was of middle height and sparsely built, his usual garb a pair of white ducks, a shirt worn outside his trousers, native-fashion, and a pair of sandals of monkey leather. He smoked evil-smelling native tobacco in a large black pipe. When he laughed, which was often, a rasping 'har! har!' he showed a nice set of blackened stumps for teeth.

He told Sandy that whenever he returned to England, he was always ill, so did tours of three or four years at a stretch on coming back to the Coast. He was immune to all diseases; he'd contracted them all, including yellow fever, a fact he was proud of as few men survive it. He'd had the clap sixteen times and thought he was naturally immune to syphilis as he'd never seen a sign of it; his knowledge and experience of the native women was, over forty years, unsurprisingly, wide and comprehensive.

The old coaster's cynical view of life and people and his fund of interesting and amusing stories, Sandy found vastly entertaining. His digestion also staggered him.

He could eat anything at any time and had a passion for what he called in the African fashion, 'chop' or hors d'oeuvres; bits and pieces of tinned salmon, sardine, potatoes with salad cream, anchovies and the like. He ate these while drinking pink gins or whiskies and then would sit down and ravenously devour his palm oil chop, chicken with ground-nuts, palm oil chips, coconut, banana, fu-fu and the rest.

Sandy was convinced he had the most unique alimentary tract in history and asked if he'd ever had gastritis.

'Me?' said Pat. 'Wot! Me? I've never 'ad a gastric stummick or a duodenal ulcer in me life! And why? Cos I eat a proper diet and never drink on an empty stummick. The mugs as consume alcohol and don't eat finish up with the D.T.'s. and your profession, Doc, are just as daft as anyone else. One doc out in the bush where I used to live tried to live on brandy and goat's milk in his later months. He wouldn't listen. Nice chap, great singer. In fact, he didn't see snakes and things when he was bad, he used to hear Handel's Messiah. And do you know, when a bloke came up from Cracra to examine the body after death he said the liver was the biggest and hardest he'd ever seen in a human corpse. Like concrete that liver was, so 'elp me. Lack o' proper diet that was!'

He was also largely indifferent to the shrieks, chirps and grunts of the busy animal night life. Nor bats, sometimes even birds, flying in, attracted by the kerosene lamp he used for illumination. Even the insect life hardly bothered him; huge moths, one species with two red gleaming eyes, great hornets fully two inches long and sometimes a large praying mantis.

One night, he told Sandy, two praying mantises dropped on to the table in front of him, one a bright green colour, the other a reddish brown. With bulging eyes and using their powerful mandibles they indulged in a mutual massacre by slowly and methodically chewing each other to pieces. Because they'd elected to enjoy this by his lamp, he got a double show from the enormous shadow they cast on the wall!

Another evening at sundown, he'd gone into his rather primitive bathroom for his usual dip in his tin tub, and there, he said, hanging from the roof, was a long evil-looking snake, glistening black with a yellow belly. He realized immediately that he was facing a Black Mamba, one of the deadliest of poisonous snakes. The reptile was curved up with its head horizontal, jaws open, forked tongue flicking rapidly, beady eyes glowing.

'Oh, I knew what to do alright.' he assured Sandy, seeing his eyes suddenly widen. 'Stay quiet, don't move if you meet any savage reptile or animal. In spite of the yarns of so-called explorers, they only attack when frightened. After a bit it just slid to the floor, ignored me and made off into the night.'

Sandy thanked him for the piece of sage advice and said he'd bear it in mind and meanwhile hope for the best.

* * *

It was proving to be very busy tour. And busy in Africa was a vastly different busy from England of course. Impossible to convey the impact and reality of the many strange diseases and tropical medical conditions rampant in the large native population, Sandy thought, never mind the somewhat hostile and frequently alarming natural environment. And of course, dealing with some difficult and even obscure cases that could not or did not respond to treatment; inevitable given some of the symptoms and that many had suffered them for too long before coming to the hospital at all.

It was different alright. But nevertheless, although frequently exhausting, he enjoyed being tested and still found it all very stimulating.

Of course, working in the oppressive heat and humidity was frequently hard going and made busy doctoring in such conditions rather a trial. The rainy season too brought its own horrors and few delights. He didn't particularly enjoy the weeks of thundering unrelenting rain and violent electric storms which seemed endless, constantly being soaked – and the noise was terrific. That it also brought on the extra complications of fungal and respiratory diseases was just something else to keep a doctor busy. He blessed his ability to sleep at the drop of a hat as the nights were ever clamourous from the insect and animal life. And of course, there were always the night time call-outs, weather conditions regardless.

The social life had its enlivening moments of course but was not very satisfactory on the purely personal level. Being by nature gregarious he'd enjoyed the company of a number of people naturally, but was perfectly happy if they passed out of his life. Though not a lot in common with colonial society, he certainly enjoyed observing it.

There was no doubt he was having a good grounding in a myriad tropical diseases. And there was definitely much to assuage his curiosity in this vastly different environment and its cultures and a considerable variety of encounters and experiences, medical and otherwise.

As the end of his tour came in sight, he thought it was time to consider whether he was going to come back for another, tempted by the chance of improving his finances further.

Then one night, agitated knocking awakened him to hurry, 'come quickly Doctor! Quickly!'

Arriving at the bungalow, he was horrified to discover the body of a young English women sprawled on the bed, covered in blood. He quickly realized that she was past help, and very recently dead. Moreover, she had been shot several times in the lower body. He recognized her as the young and very pretty wife of one of the Admin chaps. Sandy was appalled and found himself considerably disturbed by this wanton act and in such a seemingly 'civilized' circumspectly-behaved community too.

Naturally the police were called and the whole sorry tale of jealousy and murder became public knowledge. It was like a very bad taste in the mouth.

This, for some reason he couldn't quite fathom – maybe a sharp reminder of the years of torn bodies in the war – and his restless spirit, decided him. No, he would not do another tour. The prospect of England's pastures green and gentle climate surprised him by seeming like balm. He booked his passage home. He would not come back.

Chapter 17

Thanks to his West Africa tour he now had a reasonable sum in the bank. This he promised himself to try and keep intact in the hopes of improving it somehow towards that hazy goal of a practice of his own. But meanwhile it was back to getting in line at the Medical Agency in the Strand in London. At his very first visit, he walked in from seeping rain. Oh yes, he was back in England alright.

Continually on the move again through various locums he was getting to cover a considerable amount of England's green and pleasant land once more. The pattern of busy surgeries and long visiting lists was the same in virtually all these stints and for the most part the medical conditions and cases seemed common to all with some local variety thrown in. But with the constant change of faces and doctors' practices Sandy was perfectly happy.

Invariably though, the diligent locum got short shrift with every penny that came in to a practice being jealously guarded against a future when age or infirmity put paid to the doctor continuing his working life. And invariably too, as Sandy had found, the food left a great deal to be desired. Even in the country areas where he felt the fare really should have been better. For a hard-working locum, he thought with some irony, the two essentials to life, nourishment and funds, were somewhat below par.

Back in London, Sandy was given plenty of busy locums in the more crowded and least salubrious parts of the city. These doctors seemed to be more frequently in need of the temporary relief afforded by the locum set-up where the large panels and overcrowded surgeries were particularly exhausting. The pressure on their own health was considerable in these very busy practices, and how busy Sandy certainly knew from his own experience. Because malnutrition and all the ills of poverty were a pervasive addition to the prevalent diseases and umpteen medical conditions, this meant that these medicos were particularly hard-pressed.

Then after a month-long locum in a dreary Midland town, it was a relief for him when the Medical Agency asked him if he would do a locum for a doctor practicing in a Naval port on the south coast.

He was to relieve a *locum tenens* who had proved to be unsatisfactory, reasons not specified. What this might portend for himself was only conjecture of course, so, from experience, being on the qui vivre was not to be despised. The thought of the sea and fresh air though, made his acceptance unequivocal.

In no time he'd packed his bags and was off, this time to catch a train as his car, which he'd exchanged for a better one thanks to his African stint, was, pro tem, at the tender mercies of a friendly mechanic, an ex-patient to whom he'd given relief from a fine crop of boils; 'It's all the oil y'see Doctor.'

He was met off the train at the Naval Port station by a very smart car. The driver was a woman, who introduced herself as the doctor's wife, Mrs. McOwens. Much to

Sandy's alarm, she drove off rapidly bang in the middle of the road. And then alarmed Sandy further by as often as not, driving on the wrong side of the line.

She was as much occupied in driving in this erratic way as striking a series of very difficult poses with much tossing back of her fluffy hair with one hand and with the other lightly slapping the wheel. This while chattering away and asking a whole lot of questions. Was he married? Did he drink? Was he one of these troublesome locums who didn't like work and fussed about the food?

Sandy replied, No, he was not married, not especially fond of drink, not at all afraid of the work, provided, and he emphasized 'provided,' adding 'I am permitted to run the practice without any kind of unwarranted interference or advice from anyone connected to the practice except the doctor I'm replacing,' but was a bit fussy about his food. These questions dealt with he didn't feel it wise to tell her that he was so fussy about food, that he had been known to throw in the job immediately after one glance at his first meal and return by the next train, or by car which ever available.

In any case these answers had a subduing effect on Mrs. McOwens and they finished the journey in constrained silence.

As they drove, he had a chance to observe her and was pondering on what she put him in mind of. As she got out of the car and proceeded him into the house, it struck him. She was a great big, more or less, beautiful doll! A colossal doll came to mind as she was fully 5ft 9 inches tall and wearing 3 inch heels, and wearing a pink organdie frock. He'd noticed that she had a rather large bust which was now seen to be somewhat emphasized by a small waist. Her plump hips were impressive too as the organdie billowed foamily around them.

Then he took in the full impact of her head and face; the fluffy blonde hair, big blue eyes, surprised eyebrows, a little short nose, a rosebud of a mouth and pretty teeth. All exactly that of a large china doll. The whole impression at 6 feet, was quite overpowering, breathtaking even.

He was shown into a dining room, where a disconsolate young man was eyeing with very little relish, a dish of leathery-looking meat on the table before him.

'You the new man?' he asked looking up.

'Yes,' replied Sandy and dropping his voice added, 'While we are alone, do you mind giving me the low down? All I want to know is, is it the grub or the woman, or both?'

'Both.' he answered gloomily. 'But the woman is the biggest handicap. She's hounded me until I'm a nervous wreck!'

'Well, over the years I've developed a technique with troublesome wives and making them locum-conscious.'

'Well, I haven't got time to learn your technique now. I'm off as soon as I hand over to you, thank God! The doctor himself is a very decent fellow, but he's pretty sick and in hospital so not well enough to take much interest in the practice. Unfortunately, he has delegated control to Trixie, that's the big doll's name, and believe me she is as full of tricks as her cognomen! By the way,' he added, 'there's a junior partner who lives on the other side of town. He'll be in to see you shortly. He's seldom here, by the way. He and Trixie don't see eye to eye.'

An hour later his disconsolate colleague departed for another, and Sandy hoped, more amenable locum.

He was having a look at the surgery when the junior partner came in.

'I sincerely hope you will be able to stick this job,' he said. 'There's plenty to do.'

'I'll stick it,' Sandy replied, 'but why did the other chap leave?'

'Oh, Mrs. McOwen rode him too much. Made every visit an urgent one. It didn't matter what the poor bloke was doing, even in the lav she yelled at him to go at once. She revised his list, queried his prescriptions, and generally kept bothering him. He was too young and inexperienced to cope with a lady of Trixie's personality,' he said wryly. 'He started taking luminol to soothe his shattered nerves, and the other morning we couldn't rouse him. Taken a little too much of the dope. Anyway, a chap from the hospital and I managed to revive the flickering flame after some hours work and he's apparently none the worse.'

'You need have no fear of her driving me to dope but I may drive her to drink!'

'That won't be difficult,' said the junior partner, 'that is, if you pay for it. Well,' he continued, 'I'm off on my rounds, and I now leave you to her none-too tender mercies. I'll phone you one evening and you can come over to my place for a meal and meet the wife and my little family.'

Not long after he'd gone, Trixie appeared at the surgery door.

'May I come in?' she said pouting and opening her eyes at him girlishly. This did not suit her massive physique at all.

'Certainly,' he said, 'but don't stay too long. I'm going to be busy.'

This was not the reply she was hoping for and the rosebud mouth hardened. But she came in and sat down in the patient's chair.

'I'm glad of having a chance for a straight talk with you, Mrs. McOwen,' Sandy began, his voice firm but pleasant, 'as there are certain things that need to be ironed out as it were, if there is to be harmony. If my suggestions are too stringent, we had better call the whole thing off and you may be able to get a locum more amenable than I am.'

'What do you want?' she said with some asperity, dropping the babyish mein.

'I want a free hand and to be treated with the respect due to a qualified medical man, no matter if he's dubbed locum or not. Some doctors' wives,' he continued in the same reasonable tone, 'think that a man acting as *locum tenens* is a species of his own, to be treated like an unwelcome intruder or an incompetent fool. If you treat me properly, I'll treat you fair and square. Naturally I'll run your husband's practice as he would wish it done.'

'Thanks,' she said rather ungraciously. 'If your demands are reasonable, I'll go along with them, but I'll only put up with so much. Anything else?'

'Yes. I want good food,' he said, taking advantage of the opening. 'I don't mean I expect French cuisine, but plain and wholesome. No rissoles made with leftovers, no marg in place of butter, no stewed tea, or eternal fried sausages. In fact, none of the muck that is usually served up to the average locum who doesn't protest.'

'Heavens! Is that all you are interested in, food?' she cried a little scornfully.

'Not at all. I'm very fond of art, music, good literature and a host of other things.'

'All those things bore me,' she said dismissively. 'I like a good time, the pictures or theatre shows like Rose Marie and The Desert Song. My hubby likes Bach. God, how I hate that old Hun with his wearisome rattlings. If it wasn't for offending the old scout, I would smash my hubby's gramophone records with a hammer!'

'The old scout being your husband I presume,' said Sandy.

'Yes, pardon my French. But he's really good to me. Gives me anything I want and lets me do just as I please.'

Sandy didn't doubt it.

He naturally went to visit the doctor in hospital where he was recovering from appendicitis. As well as a courtesy, it was his practice and there were naturally things to mention since he wasn't on hand to be kept informed.

He found Dr McOwen to be a man of Herculean physique, well-suited, Sandy thought to his wife's considerable proportions. He had strongly-marked features and a long chin and dry fusty-looking hair which was thinning on top. Sandy found him to be a kindly uncomplicated man who expressed himself as grateful to Sandy for looking after his busy practice.

One day Mrs. McOwen confided to Sandy that she was very worried as her son was coming home. Sandy had no idea she had a child. 'Oh, haven't you seen his photo in the drawing room?'

'I've never been into the drawing room, no occasion to,' Sandy replied.

'Well, come and have a look, it's all my own décor,' she smiled happily, leading the way into the room. He followed and fairly blinked in astonishment. Black cane furniture, a pink carpet, floral cushions, a settee ornamented with pink bows and pink roses rioting over the wall-paper. The whole chocolate box effect suited her very well, he thought, schooling his features as best he could. She didn't notice though as she had crossed the room to point out a large picture over the mantelpiece. It was an enlargement of a photograph. 'This is my son Cyril,' she said.

It was obvious from the vacant eyes and expression that the boy was of concern to his parents.

'Poor Cyril,' she said. 'His brain is not fully developed, well, only partially,' she explained, 'but we found a special school for him where they would do the best for him and stimulate his brain as much as possible. But he's 17 now and has of course developed physically if you know what I mean and, er, and doesn't seem quite able to…well anyway he has developed certain sexual interests that they are finding difficult to deal with, so they have asked us to take him away from the school.' It was obvious she was awaiting her son's arrival with some misgiving.

Sandy said he would try to help her son, but was quite unprepared for the young giant who arrived the following day. Cyril was also accompanied by a huge amount of luggage. He was well over 6 feet, broadly built and well-dressed in a plus four tweed suit. It was very smart but made him appear even more overpowering. He was also bald and had his mother's large blue eyes but they were vacant and lashless. But the special school had obviously been good for him as he was well-mannered and pleasant and seemed happy.

The school, Trixie said, had reported that his sexual offences were mild but upsetting to the female staff. Unfortunately, Cyril had been bought a camera by his mother; the psychiatrist having looked at Cyril's enterprising photographs of the girls he had, it transpired, bribed to remove their clothing, had tried and then failed to allay the lad's curiosity. The school felt that it would be better if he left. From the description of his activities Sandy said they certainly sounded more like curiosity than anything serious.

At home Cyril was easily bored and as a result his mother kept buying him things to amuse and divert him, including of all things, puzzled Sandy, a very good typewriter. He started to spend more time away from home and Trixie supplied him with plenty of money – which Sandy discretely advised against. His mother wasn't unduly concerned as he didn't stay out late and always came home for his tea saying he had been looking at the ships or going to the pictures.

Then one day he staggered them by announcing that he was engaged to be married. At first Trixie thought this was a joke. But no, her name was Jenny Dilnot and her father worked at the gas works.

Sandy started. He remembered Jenny. She was a little undersized for her 15 years and he had immediately realised, not very bright. Her father had brought her to the surgery to ask for something to 'pep her up a bit Doc.' Being a new doctor perhaps he might know of something for her? Sandy guessed he was hoping this would improve matters but said that he would prescribe a good tonic being in his view the only help he could offer.

After announcing the astonishing piece of news of his engagement and devouring his usual enormous meal with great gusto, Cyril left. Sandy then told Trixie about Jenny. Now greatly alarmed, she wondered how on earth she was to tell her husband. He suggested they visit the Dilnots to see if the engagement was in fact, true.

'Yes, straight away! We must get a move on as I bet that's where he's off to,' she cried and rushed from the house. Once in the car, she drove at top speed, in an effort to cut Cyril off.

What ensued was memorable.

Unfortunately, Cyril with a camera and a complaisant girl were not a good combination. And the expensive presents he used as bribes and rewards for the girl, pleased her parents no end.

Sandy and the agitated Trixie found the dilapidated cottage at the docks adjoining the gas works. When they arrived, Cyril was already seated in the rather low-ceilinged kitchen as was young Jenny who was fondling an expensive-looking piano-accordion which was rather too big for her. Also in the untidy fusty room, lit only by its one small window, sat Mr Dilnot in his shirt-sleeves, eating and still unwashed after his coke-shoveling morning and Mrs. Dilnot, an undersized grey-haired and untidy female, stirring something on the stove.

This touching scene alas, obviously did not appeal itself to Mrs. McOwen who strode up to the mantelpiece where there were two silver-framed photos one of Cyril and the other of Jenny. Seizing both pictures, she flung them to the ground with a crash. Jenny immediately screeched out a loud protest in very obscene language, while her mother wanted to know. 'Wot the 'ell she thought she was a-doin' of?'

A regular racket ensued; the doctor's wife seizing her large son's arm and attempting to drag him away while Cyril roared that he wasn't going to leave his girlfriend. Mr. Dilnot, with his mouth full of food shouted explosively that he would bung them all out, while Mrs Dilnot shrieked that Mrs. McOwen was no lady. Sandy somehow managed to suggest in the midst of this din that they all sit down and have a friendly talk. Thankfully this appealed to Mrs. Dilnot, so order was soon restored. Mrs. McOwen meanwhile, sat glaring balefully at Jenny perched on her chair swinging her legs, fiddling with the stops on the accordion and pressing the keys in random order. The result was far from melodious. Sandy kept in the background, leaning on the now empty mantelpiece and wondering if he was in a madhouse or a comic opera.

Mrs. Dilnot told his mother and Sandy that Cyril had met their Jenny at the fairground near the docks and had treated her to 'all the rides and everything!'

It transpired that they'd then gone off to a disused shed where he had pursued the anatomical investigations he so delighted in until they had been disturbed, luckily by a workman who knew Jenny's father.

As Mrs. Dilnot went on to tell Trixie all about it, the tale that unfolded revealed, that thanks to all the expensive gifts and even 'lovely family outings,' Cyril was made very welcome and visited often. They were flattered by the attentions of a doctor's son for their Jenny and impressed by his largesse.

Mr Dilnot then related with some amusement the visit to the photographers to have Jenny's picture taken. Apparently, she had jibbed at the camera and refused to look pleasant and when the photographer said, 'smile please!' she had astonished the man by shouting, 'Smile yer bloody self!' which Mr. Dilnot obviously thought hilarious. Mrs. Dilnot then pitched in with the tale of their visit afterwards to a posh hotel lounge for tea as a treat from dear Cyril, but Jenny's language and naughty behaviour upset the other people there so the manager told them all 'to get out and be quick about it!'

Then some days after the outing Mrs. Dilnot herself came home and found Cyril at his researches with their daughter. She told him that if these goings on were to continue he must marry Jenny or at least become engaged. Cyril was very happy with this idea and turned up the next day she said, with a 'real nice engagement ring,' and went over to lift up Jenny's non-too-clean finger for inspection.

Trixie was horrified. The beautiful diamond and sapphire ring was her very own. 'That's mine!' she shrilled, jumping to her feet, trembling with rage and tears starting from her eyes. Turning on her son, her mouth quivering with her pent-up emotions, she wept, 'You stole that from my jewellery box! You *stole* it! You great lumbering lummox! I've a damn good mind to let you stew in your own juice and marry that awful girl!'

Cyril wasn't a bit put out and grinned slyly and said, 'Okay, Mama. Okay.'

Grim-faced, Trixie made for the door and asked Sandy to drive her straight to the hospital. She needed to tell her husband immediately of this dreadful affair.

On the way Sandy pointed out that marriage was out of the question, they were well underage and even tried to reassure her that it was extremely unlikely that anyone could be found to marry them. Trixie was not mollified in the least.

The doctor nearly burst his stitches when he heard the stories of his son's amorous adventures, 'and the girl barely more than a child!' There was only one thing to be done. Cyril had to go to a suitable home where he could be kept away from pursuing any more such activities, he said.

The Doctor silenced Trixie's protests and said it really must be done, pointing out to her the considerable difficulties as Cyril grew older, undoubtedly even less possible to supervise or influence. And this must be dealt with as soon as possible; they might be involved in an unsavoury court case if the Dilnots cut up rough and reported Cyril's research work with the child.

Highly likely, thought Sandy, with Cyril's lovely fund of money drying up; Trixie would definitely cut his money to practically nil. The thought must have occurred to

Trixie too who cried that she was damned well not funding Cyril and the Dilnots till he came of age!

It had to be through the offices of the Junior partner and Sandy that everything was arranged and as quickly as possible.

Cyril only realized when he got there that this was where he was now going to live and without Jenny. But they very kindly took him in charge. Sandy couldn't help but feel heart-sorry for the lad but had to agree that there was nothing else to be done and that it was the safest place for him to be. He had previously been quite happy away from home at the other place. Anyway, thought Sandy ruefully, it was patently obvious that the responsibility was quite beyond Trixie. Combined with the doctor running a full-time practice, it would be impossible to either watch out for or prevent any further excursions into the researches so absorbing to their very large and determined son.

⧐ Chapter 18⧏

Except for a slight depression of spirits lasting a few days, the ignominious career of her son and his release from her parental care had little effect on one of Trixie's superficial nature.

Shortly after, her spirits rose when she announced one lunch time, 'The Fleet's in,' smiling happily and obviously full of anticipation. Trixie's life had suddenly brightened considerably.

She had seen the grey shapes of the destroyers coming into the harbour as she motored home from her shopping trip. She hoped 'The Shrike' was amongst the arrivals as the Commander she said, was a great friend of hers.

'Ooh! I must go down and see if it has come in! I can't wait! Would you like to come too? – as a chaperon of course!' she smiled engagingly, doll-like face aglow.

Sandy agreed to accompany her down to the docks later that afternoon to find out. He should have finished his visiting list by tea-time he assured her, so he'd be free before evening surgery.

After tea Trixie went off upstairs in high spirits to get dolled-up.

She came down wreathed in smiles in a confection of pale blue organdie with a wide-brimmed hat of tulle trimmed with cornflowers and those very high heels, looking more doll-like than ever. Her golden curls bobbing beside her face and a quantity of makeup completed the picture to a high degree.

Golly! thought Sandy, this'll go down well with the sailing fraternity alright!

'How do I look?' she asked, blue eyes sparkling and rosebud mouth pouting with anticipation.

'Marvelous!' said Sandy, 'You'll knock 'em in the Old Kent Road al' right!'

'Don't be vulgar. What I mean is, will the boys like it?'

'If you mean the Navy boys,' he replied, 'there's no doubt about it!'

Giggling with delight she went past him and out to the car, exuding a cloud of perfume and face powder, blue organdie billowing out and around her.

Viewing all six foot of this amazing sight, Sandy felt positive that even the most sophisticated sailor would not fail to be impressed with this beautiful, though outsized, doll.

At the dock gates, the guard seemed to know her and waved them through without a word. They drew up alongside a fleet of destroyers, anchored beam to beam with gangways connecting one to the other.

Emerging from the car like Venus from the foam, Trixie trotted off to look for the 'Shrike' emblem on one of them, Sandy following behind. She spotted it the third out from the dockside and exclaimed with delight. She reached it then ran nimbly up its gangway, organdie billowing and high heels clicking merrily as she went.

Sandy followed her up more slowly and found her on the deck being greeted by her Commander friend. He was a tall good-looking man about Sandy's age. His dark hair was only lightly streaked with grey; just enough to make him look distinguished. By his expression, he was obviously deriving considerable enjoyment from Trixie's appearance.

He invited them down to the wardroom for drinks. Perfectly happy to do so, Sandy followed them down. Drinks were ordered and he was introduced to the others including the First Officer, Anderson.

'A fellow Scot!' he greeted him, smiling, 'and here's another for you!' and hailed another officer just entering in their wake. He was the Medical Officer, Peterson, and was immediately introduced to Sandy.

'And fellow Aberdonian!' cried a delighted Sandy, smiling at the familiar accent greeting him back.

They were much of an age and plunged into conversation straight away, Sandy's nearly English voice slipping back into his native accent and vernacular with ease. They were on first name terms with the first drink and yarning about varsity days.

Sandy had evening surgery, so invited him back to the house, always glad to meet a colleague but as welcome conversational relief. Trixie was all aglow and perfectly safe he felt being the centre of attention in the crowded wardroom. In any case she was the Commander's responsibility, not his.

Later in the course of their conversation Sandy did make reference to Trixie and the Commander. Yes, it was all perfectly innocent, Peterson said. The skipper was a happily married man. His wife was recuperating rather slowly from a serious operation in a local nursing home where he visited her when he could. His attitude towards Trixie was more paternal than anything else.

Sandy was glad to hear it. He liked Dr McOwen and felt he had enough worries. His recovery was being a little slow but Sandy reckoned the usual doctor's complaint of exhaustion had something to do with it.

For several days he caught only fleeting glimpses of Trixie. She spent most of her time at the dockyard or going to dances or the pictures with her sailor. To keep all things snug and ship-shape, she did take her gallant Commander to visit her husband in the hospital. He had met him before and had no objection to his friendship with Trixie.

The Naval doc Alan Peterson and Sandy got about a bit too in his spare time and enjoyed the hospitality for which the Navy is justly famed. Sandy felt happy and at home with these sailormen. He wondered if it was that the Navy had their drinks duty free or was it simply their tradition behind it? He hadn't found the Army so convivial.

He was enjoying himself immensely in the little wardroom where the company was bright and breezy. On his day off, Alan invited him to what he called 'a slight binge.'

One young man with one ring of gold braid on his arm attracted Sandy's attention as he sat with down-cast eyes and silently throughout the entire meal. He looked very young. He was very English with fair hair and clear pale skin and neat rather refined features.

Sandy felt he wanted to discover the cause of his obvious depression so sought an opportunity to sit next to him. This he managed to do and sat down with his coffee and liqueur to engage him in conversation.

Gently remarking that all did not seem well in his world, the young man responded by silently drawing a cutting from his pocket and handing it to Sandy. The press cutting described how a Naval captain had been found shot in his cabin some hours before he was due to face a court-martial for some offence.

'He was my best friend on the ship,' said the young officer, 'and now they have driven him to his death.'

'What was the offence that he was going to be tried for?' asked Sandy. The boy did not answer but begged to be excused and left the wardroom. Trixie's Commander came over and sat next to Sandy and addressed him with a grin on his attractive face. 'Doing a bit of psycho-analytical stuff Doc?'

'No, I was only curious about the lad's obvious depression.'

'Well, if you want to know the reason for the Captain's sudden demise, I'll tell you. The old story I'm afraid. Liked pretty boys instead of pretty girls and was found out. *In flagrante* actually and couldn't face the music, so, took the easy way out,' he said a trifle wryly. 'Don't think I'm admitting that that sort of thing is any more common in the Navy than in Civil or Ecclesiastical life because it isn't, in spite of popular belief. But it is bound to occur when men are so much thrown together and more especially since men like that do exist.'

Sandy agreed with the Commander but failed to find any answer to this sad state of affairs.

'Anyway, the Navy at sea has no choice but to endure sexual starvation of course,' the Commander grinned, 'or render ourselves impotent with cheap gin.' Sandy realized that he was half-joking and half-serious. 'But I imagine you're too busy to worry much about women when you are at sea.'

'Mostly, thank God,' smiled the Commander, 'but at times one does rather miss the company of the fair sex.'

Just then a great burst of laughter ended their conversation; the room was becoming a bedlam. Chaps from other ships drifted in jamming up the doorway and overflowing into the companionway. Men also from the Fleet Air Arm mingled with the jostling and increasingly merry crowd. Everyone was having the time of their lives and Sandy felt completely in his element with this exuberant crowd, full of pep-talk and physical well-being with their loud and laughing voices proclaiming their disregard for the future.

In a few years from then, the day when the Sharnhorst was attacked by the Fleet Air Arm, he thought of those young flyers, mere boys who had laughed and drunk with him, flying straight into the enemy flak with their inferior machines and sub-sized torpedoes.

Later in the evening a few charming women arrived including Trixie. She had been to the hospital visiting her husband she said, like a dutiful wife. She'd brought with her a friend who the sailors immediately dubbed The Musical Box. She was there to play the piano she said, whenever a piano was available.

Sandy lost no time in asking her if he could get her a drink. She was very pretty with a delicious smile and said yes, gin with lime juice. 'They say if you drink gin with lime juice you don't get a hangover,' she said and toasted him with her drink, smiling sweetly, her brown eyes looking him over. There was no room to sit down so they stood drinking and chatting, talking about music and various other topics.

She soon found he was a doctor but Sandy adroitly steered her away from that subject. He said it took up too much of his life so wanted to think of more charming things. Just then the First Officer squeezed through the throng and said he'd ordered a few taxis for those willing to take part in a binge. A very well-known scientific woman had a big house on a headland overlooking the sea some miles from the port and always left her keys when she wasn't in residence for any officers off the ships to use certain of the rooms for dancing and jollification.

The taxis arrived and they all packed in, giggling girls and laughing officers with a sprinkling of slightly more serious chaps like Sandy, who in truth favoured watching other people whom he found endlessly enthralling. On the way they stopped at a pub where a good cargo of drink was shipped on board then away again making all speed for the house on the headland.

On arrival and after the fug of the taxi, the headland air felt refreshing and cool. Sandy immediately attached himself to the delectable Musical Box whose name was Penny. She tucked her arm in his and they strolled over to look at the sea and inhaled the glorious air. The moon, most obligingly, was up and flooded the sea with platinum light.

Before Sandy could take any advantage of this, she heard her name called and said she must go and do her duty as the Musical Box.

They headed for the house where by the sound of things the party was in full swing. They arrived in time to save the grand piano from being swamped by the dregs from sundry beer bottles which a merry matelot was watering the strings. As Penny sat down, this was a signal for the piano to be cleared of the detritus of all glasses and bottles.

The girl played for hours. Syncopation, waltzes, songs interspersed with classical music, Mozart, Liszt, all un-noticed by the throng fully engaged in smoking, opening bottles, necking, and such dancing as they were capable of. Amid yells for the pianist to keep to this or that rhythm, fox trot, rumba, the atmosphere getting thicker with cigarette smoke, Penny played on in this pandemonium like a somnambulist, barely pausing now and then for a fresh gin and lime then resuming her musical peregrinations.

Sandy hadn't had a chance to speak to her and was getting a trifle bored with a long rambling discourse from some chap about Duke Ellington. Also, he wasn't participating in the necking and dancing and interesting conversation was definitely at a premium.

Seizing a moment when she paused to refresh herself but still continued playing with the other hand, Sandy went over and suggested Penny take a break. 'The mob are only using you as a background,' he said. 'I know,' she replied, 'but I'm inured to the fact by now and I don't mind. They wouldn't enjoy themselves so much without it so I just carry on and I do enjoy it.' So skilled was she that she continued playing as she was talking to him.

'Can't I persuade you to at least get a breath of fresh air?' he asked.

'Can't do it Doc. If I stop, everything stops, I've tried it before. If I cease this racket, the conversation dies down and the crowd look blank, they begin to wonder what's happened, everything hangs fire. Can't spoil the party now Doc!'

She was hiding it well but he could see she was weary and he was getting a little concerned. He eventually found a lieutenant who was willing to give her a break, even if he could only play by ear so persuaded her to give up her seat to him for a spell. As they left them to it no-one seemed to notice the change and everyone just carried on with the party.

He steered her out into the fresh air and made for the headland and the soft grass there. They sat down and he saw that her expression as she gazed out at the sea was pensive and distracted.

'Peaceful isn't it?' she said. 'The matelots are saying it won't be peaceful for long. The Nazi's are spoiling for a fight and the Naval chaps seem all for a scrap.' She then admitted she'd fallen for a lieutenant Muir who was in the Fleet Air Arm. She was mad about him. Sandy had met him and remembered conversations with him on their mutual love of classical music. He was a very keen pilot. 'But,' she said, 'he's not keen on me Doc. In fact, he's actually cold towards me and I can't understand why he's so distant!' She sighed. 'Perhaps it's as well really. If there *is* going to be a war, he'll be right in the thick of it. Do you think that's why? No ties just in case?'

Before Sandy could offer any sort of consoling words there were unmistakable sounds behind them of the party breaking up so they got up and joined them. He found Trixie looking a little disheveled and swore she'd been looking for him everywhere to drive her home; she had been out for a drive with the Commander in the doctor's car but had refused to allow her escort to drive her home in case the neighbours' would talk and gracious! It was two in the morning!

The lights went out as the few more or less sober ones locked up. The taxis and cars had begun to arrive and the Navy and their charming company made off into the night.

The doctor's wife was in great form on the return home and on arrival even offered to make Sandy some coffee. Had he had a good time? she asked? She had! That was the life, company, dancing, music!

'God what a life I led until I met the Navy! My hubby Charles, you know, he's a good sort and all that but he doesn't know anything about how to enjoy himself. His idea of fun is going fishing or watching a football match! Not jazz or dancing! When I tell him the funniest stories I've heard from the Navy boys, he just looks at me and says, 'Just so. – Just so?' she shrilled, 'What do you make of that, I ask you?'

Sandy replied that he couldn't make anything of it especially at this hour; he was off to bed. He wished her goodnight and left her in the kitchen with the coffee pot and her fulminations.

He was awakened in what he thought was the middle of the night by the phone ringing beside his bed. He reached blearily for the receiver. Not a call out, good! but heard instead the voice of the Commander who asked for Mrs. McOwen.

Realising now that it was actually morning, Sandy got up and, and leaving Trixie chatting away excitedly to her Commander, set about his day; three surgeries, and no doubt the usual busy list of visits and several private patients to keep happy for the doctor.

Two days later Dr McOwen himself returned home ready to work, bringing Sandy's locum to the usual abrupt end.

* * *

Sandy leaned on the taffrail, watching the harbour slip away as the ship headed into the open sea. Smiling, he smoothed the two rings of gold braid with the strip of red velvet between. Surgeon Lieutenant R.N. No more Medical Agency he thought with an inward cheer. After ten years of practicing medicine, a salaried doctor at last.

These were challenging times and war was brewing, so who knew what lay before him on those tumbling seas to satisfy that restless adventurous spirit of his? Perhaps, he thought, this was his metier at last – out on the seas – 'the 'bounding main.' The movement, the freedom, the open skies, the sea a restless counterpart to himself. And the whole world before him.

Useful abbreviations and terms

4

M.B.Ch.B. - Bachelor of Medicine.(deg) Bachelor of Surgery.(deg) (Ch was short for Chirurgery the old name for surgery from the Greek, Kheirurgia – ergo a surgeon was a chirurgeon.)

F.R.C.S. - Fellow of the Royal College of Surgeons.

F.R.C.P – Fellow of the Royal College of Physicians.

M.D. - Doctor of Medicine.

M.R.C.P. - Master of the Royal College of Physicians.

L.R.C.S. – Licensed Respiratory Care Practitioner.

M.R.C.S - Membership of Royal College of Surgeons post grad diploma.

M.R.C.G. – Membership of the Royal College of Gænacologists

L.C.C. – London County Council.

BMA. – British Medical Association.

D.T's – *Dilirium Tremens.* The physiological state of severe delirium and trembling due to chronic alcoholism.